A Lesson on Love

by

Sharon C. Cooper

Dedication

To my biggest fans, my mom and dad, Willie and Johnnie Mae Cunningham. Thanks for your endless support and encouragement over the years. Love you two so much! *Muah!*

Chapter One

Jerry Jenkins turned his head left and right, tugging on the irritating bow-tie before lifting the glass of whiskey to his lips. His groomsman duties were over, and he couldn't wait to shed his tuxedo.

But right now, he stared out at the dance floor where his cousin Nate and his new bride, Liberty, danced their first dance. Brian McKnight's *The Only One for Me* poured through the hotel ballroom speakers as the couple stared into each other's eyes, smiling as if they were the only two people in the room. Jerry didn't miss the way Liberty gazed up at Nate. Like he hung the moon. Like there was no one in the world that she'd rather be with.

A stab of jealousy pierced his chest. He had never been envious of anyone. He always got what he wanted—including women. Yet, watching the newlyweds brought home what he was missing in his life. Someone to call his own.

That was a first. He loved and respected women, but never wanted to be tied down to just one.

At least not until recently.

Not until a certain beauty moved in next door to him.

Jerry held back a groan bubbling in his throat as thoughts of his neighbor infiltrated his mind...again. He couldn't shake the unrest stirring in his chest.

1

Damn, this is messed up.

He wanted Rayne Ellison in a way he never wanted another woman. Maybe he'd been around too many loving couples lately. Seems so many of the Jenkins family members were happily tying the knot. Was he really ready for a lifetime commitment with one woman?

"Dance with me."

Jerry glanced to his left, caught off guard by the melodious words that had been spoken close to his ear. *That voice.* He took in the statuesque goddess with her long, straight hair hanging past her shoulders, tawny brown skin with minimum makeup, and a smile that could be featured in a toothpaste commercial. To say she was stunning in the strapless royal blue dress that hugged her curvaceous body would be an understatement.

But he felt nothing. The usual stirring that would have once had him leading her past the dance floor and to the nearest dark corner to make out wasn't there.

"I hate turning down a beautiful woman," he finally said. "But I'm going to have to pass."

"That's too bad." Her bold fingers traced a path down his arm while she stared into his eyes. "I would love to have had the pleasure of finally being in the arms of the infamous Jerry Jenkins."

Normally he would have appreciated her boldness, but her comment grated on his nerves. For months he'd been trying to shake his lady's man reputation. Yet, someone always found a way to remind him that it's tough living down a reputation.

"Not tonight, Lo…" He stopped short of calling her *Love*, a term he often used with women. If he ever expected for people to believe he'd changed, he needed to chill with the terms of endearment that often flew from his mouth when he didn't know a woman's name.

"You sure you don't want to dance?"

"Positive."

After a slight hesitation, she dropped her hand from his arm and gave a shrug before sauntering off. Instead of watching her walk away, like he used to do, Jerry slammed back the rest of his drink.

"What the hell? I'm standing right next to you. Am I invisible or something?" Liam Jenkins, Jerry's cousin, grumbled over the music. "That's the fourth woman in the past twenty minutes who has asked you to dance. Yet, not one looked my way. I could see if you were better looking than me, but that's not the case."

Jerry chuckled. They'd had similar conversations like this one. He leaned against the bar where they stood and held up his empty glass, signaling the bartender for a refill. He and Liam had been mistaken for brothers more than once, despite Jerry being a shade darker with less facial hair. At thirty, almost two years older than Jerry, Liam was six feet tall with a runner's build. Jerry had a few inches on him and was a good twenty-five pounds heavier.

"What can I say, man? Women love me. It's a gift." *Or a curse*, he thought the moment the words were out of his mouth. Since the third grade, he had never had trouble snagging the attention of the opposite sex. A serial dater for most of his adult life, he had come by his reputation of loving women, honestly. He wasn't a jerk about it. He treated the ladies well and with respect, leaving them wanting more of his attention.

Liam leaned in closer. "What's even more mind-boggling is that you've turned down every woman, and two of them were definitely your type. Thick and curvy. Heck, I've seen the time when you'd be out on the dance floor with two or three honeys at the same time. So, what's wrong with you?"

Accepting the whiskey from the bartender, Jerry swirled the glass before bringing it to his lips. No, it wasn't like him to turn down a woman. But his world changed a few months ago when Rayne's fine ass strolled into his life. He hadn't been right since. He only wanted her.

The scary part was that his attraction to Rayne wasn't just about looks. He'd admit to being somewhat shallow in the past, but he liked everything about her. They had quickly become friends. Laughing, talking and joking with each other as if they'd known each other for years. Gorgeous and smart with just enough sass, Rayne also had something else going for her. She was an amazing mom to the sweetest little girl that had stolen Jerry's heart the moment their eyes met.

"There you go staring off into space again," Liam said, interrupting Jerry's musings. "So what? Nothing to say?"

Jerry shrugged and turned to face the crowded ballroom and leaned his back against the bar. "What do you want me to say?"

"I wanna know what's going on with you. I want to know…" His words trailed off and Jerry didn't have to look at him to know that he was staring at him. "Wait. Don't tell me that this *new you* has something to do with that neighbor lady."

Even if he couldn't go a few minutes without thinking about Rayne, Jerry wasn't in the mood to discuss her. The only reason some of the people in his family even knew she existed was because of Nate. His cousin had stopped by Jerry's house months ago and like a fool, Jerry had told him about his feelings for Rayne. Soon after, the Jenkins family's rumor mill was in full swing. For months he'd had to deal with some of his cousins ragging him about him finally falling for *the one*.

"Tell me about her."

Jerry gave Liam a sidelong glance, trying to determine if he was really interested in knowing more about Rayne, or if he was just setting him up to be the butt of some joke. Had it been one of his other cousins, Jerry would've assumed the latter, but Liam was different. Unlike some of the others, who lived to dish out bullshit, Liam was more serious and understanding.

"Her name is Rayne, and yes, she's my neighbor. I can't figure her out. Each time I ask her on a date, she shoots me down."

Liam nodded, looking as if he was in deep thought before speaking. "I've never known you to get caught up with any one woman. I'm surprised you haven't moved on. What's so special about this one?"

"Everything," Jerry said shrugging, unable to keep the awe out of his tone. "There's no moving on from her. She's the one for me."

Liam's mouth dropped open slowly as he continued to stare at him. Seconds of his silence ticked by. Then he burst out laughing. "Yeah, right. Until the next *one* comes along."

Oh, here we go. So much for thinking they could have an adult conversation.

Jerry tuned him out and went back to studying the crowd of individuals. Immediately following the wedding ceremony, Nate and Liberty had hosted a sit-down dinner for just family. That was a few hours ago. Now the reception they were all currently at was basically a party for all of those who hadn't been invited to the dinner.

Nate and Liberty had spared no expense for their wedding day. The buffet tables on each side of the banquet room were loaded with food. Jerry couldn't eat another bite if he wanted to. Now he stood at one of the two partial cash bars drowning his sorrows.

Liam finally sobered, looking at Jerry as if seeing him for the first time. "Wait. You're serious?"

"Very," Jerry said dryly.

"I thought you said you loved women too much to ever settle down with just one."

"That was before I found one worth settling down with." Heck, he'd said a lot of things over the years that he wasn't proud of, but he was older and wiser now.

Liam nodded, still studying Jerry. "This must be serious. Why didn't you bring her to the wedding?"

"I asked. She turned me down. I can't get the woman to take me seriously. She might be new to the city, but she's heard that I date… a lot. Well, used to."

"I guess your Casanova reputation has caught up to you and not in a good way."

Jerry straightened, trying to keep his frustration at bay. "Man, that's just it. I've changed. She hasn't seen women coming in and out of my house because I haven't been out with anyone. But she won't give me a chance to prove that I'm not the same man."

They stood in silence, and Jerry returned his attention to the dance floor. Some of the guests showed off their smooth moves, while others sat at the round tables eating and drinking. Then there were some standing around talking and laughing. Everyone seemed to be having a good time while he wallowed in self-pity.

"Man, I can't believe it. Maybe there really is something to the Jenkins' men myth?"

Jerry narrowed his eyes. "What myth?"

"You seriously don't know?"

Jerry shook his head not having a clue to what he was talking about.

"The Jenkins' men myth is…wait. Actually, even as the horndog of the family, you might've just proved that it's not a myth. If a woman can get and hold your attention, there might be something to this. Anyway, it's been said that when a Jenkins man meets *the one*, he immediately knows. Even if he tries to walk away or denies his feelings for the woman, it doesn't matter. They're destined to be together."

Jerry studied him, trying to determine if his cousin was serious. Liam met his stare head on. "You've got to be kidding. Who came up with that, Gram?" he asked of their grandmother, Katherine Jenkins, the backbone of the family. "You know what? Maybe it is true. All I know is that whenever I'm near Rayne, I can't think straight. She throws me off my game every time. Now all I want is for her to give me a chance to prove I've changed."

"Well, I'm not an expert on women, but I do know one thing."

"What's that?"

"You can talk all you want about how you've changed, or how you're no longer a player, but a woman ain't tryin' to hear all that. If you're serious about the neighbor lady, you're going to have to *show her* who you really are, who you want her to see when she sees you."

Jerry considered all that his cousin was saying. He was definitely serious about wanting more than a friendship with Rayne. For the first time it wasn't about getting a woman into his bed. It was about getting the right woman, her, to be a part of his life.

Now, all he had to do was figure out how to make that a reality.

Chapter Two

Past due.
Second notice.

Rayne Ellison's chest tightened as she stared down at the pile of past due bills on the kitchen counter. Her gaze went to the electric bill in her hand, the words *second notice* blurring because of the tears filling her eyes. It didn't matter how many hours she put in at work, she never seemed to have enough cash.

Was it too much to wish for one month where she didn't have to figure out how to stretch money? Lately, it seemed to be one surprise expense after another. A couple of weeks ago, she'd had to replace the radiator in her old Chevy after putting it off for months. At the rate she was going, before long, she would have replaced everything on the car.

Rayne dropped the bill onto the counter and closed her eyes to push away the emotion threatening to overpower her. She couldn't keep going like this. Three years since her husband's death, and still she struggled financially. If only Kirk hadn't left her with a mound of debt and no life insurance.

Anger crept through her body. It wasn't good to think ill of the dead, but she despised everything about the man. The lack of respect, the cheating, and then leaving her with bills she hadn't known existed, made her hate him that much more. It was bad enough that he'd been a crappy husband towards the end of their relationship, but the shit that hit the fan after his death would forever haunt her.

Rayne shook her head. *I'm not going there.* Kirk had already robbed her of her belief in happily ever after. No way would she allow herself to go to that dark place in her mind. Besides, it was her fault for giving up so much of her independence to the wrong man. She'd been a fool back then, but never again. Never would she give a man the chance to destroy her self-confidence...or her life.

Her gaze returned to the stack of bills. Something had to give. Rayne had hoped living in a new city would provide a good job and a fresh start. But so far, she was still struggling to make ends meet with her factory job that paid just a little more than minimum wage. Some days she just wanted to throw up her hands and say, *I quit. I give up. I...*

"Mommy, can we go to the bookstore?"

Rayne startled. With the heel of her hand, she quickly dabbed at the corners of her eyes not wanting her over observant five-year-old to see her upset. Stormy had been so quiet in the adjourning living room watching television that Rayne had momentarily forgotten that she wasn't alone.

She glanced down at her daughter. The two long ponytails on each side of her child's head were frizzy and in need of brushing, but they didn't detract from her cuteness. They framed her adorable face that was the color of deep amber, but it was the innocent, light-brown eyes staring up at Rayne that made her heart turn to mush.

A smile tugged up the corners of Rayne's lips. This little person who depended on her for everything was the reason she kept going and refused to give up. No matter how dismal life seemed at times, her daughter had a way of brightening the cloudiest day. Instead of naming her Stormy, a more appropriate name would've been Sunshine.

"How about we go to the library instead?" Rayne finally said.

Just finishing up in pre-k, Stormy was reading at a first-grade level and Rayne wanted to continue feeding both of their love for books and reading. She had hoped to have a little extra money from her check to buy them each a new book. That wasn't going to happen. Now she was glad she hadn't made any promises.

"And then can we get some ice cream?"

"Stormy, it's nine o'clock in the morning, way too early for ice cream."

"Oh. Can we go later then?"

"We'll see."

At least she hadn't asked about getting new shoes. Rayne had enrolled her into an all-day summer program at a nearby daycare center and the first day was in three weeks. That meant she had a little time before she had to buy her baby new gym shoes since kids weren't allowed to wear sandals to the center.

All wasn't bad, though. Rayne had found out a week earlier that the state would pay the majority of the child care fee for the summer.

Now I just have to scrape up enough cash for shoes and these other bills.

"Are we gettin' ready to go?" Stormy asked, sliding back and forth around the kitchen floor in her Minnie Mouse furry footies.

"Yes, as soon as you go upstairs and get your sandals."

"Okay." Her daughter took off for the stairs.

Rayne gathered the bills from the top of the laminate countertop and stuffed them into the wicker basket that she usually kept on the top shelf of the pantry.

She glanced around the first floor of the townhouse. Leaving San Antonio and moving to Cincinnati six months ago had been the best decision she'd made in a long time. She owed it all to her high school best friend, Charlee Fenlon. Thanks to Charlee, Rayne had landed a job at a factory and connected with the landlord of the townhome. For the first couple of months, he had given her a sizeable discount on the rent, and then recently, she had qualified for rent assistance. The subsidy was a godsend. Otherwise, there was no way she'd be able to afford the place which was located in a beautiful, safe neighborhood. But even with the financial help, some months of trying to cover past and present bills were still tough.

"I'm done, Mommy," Stormy called out as she came down the stairs and trotted into the kitchen. "Can I take Bunny with me?" She held up the pink stuffed animal.

"Sure, but you'll have to keep up with him." Rayne grabbed her purse. "All right, kiddo. Let's get going."

"Can I say hi to Jerry first? Please."

Rayne didn't know what her daughter's infatuation was with Jerry Jenkins, their next-door neighbor. Then again, yes, she did. Jerry was a charmer. It didn't matter the age of the female, they all drooled over his good looks and captivating disposition. She and Stormy were no different. Both had fallen under his stupid spell, and that frustrated Rayne more than her attraction to him. No, it was more than an ordinary attraction. A combustible sexual tension vibrated between them whenever they were within ten feet of each other.

Rayne wanted to believe that she wasn't affected by the handsome man, but who was she kidding? She wanted to see him as much as Stormy did. The only difference was Rayne knew his type. There was no way she was losing herself to another player.

"Maybe later, Stormy. Right now, we need to run some errands and then we'll head to the library."

Her daughter poked out her bottom lip. "But Mommy. He—"

"What did I say?" This was one of those days that Rayne didn't feel like repeating herself or participating in any negotiating with a five-year-old.

"You said maybe later," Stormy mumbled, as she held her bunny in a choke hold.

They silently headed to the door and stepped outside. The moment Rayne locked up, Jerry's door swung open and his keys jingled. What were the chances they'd be leaving home at the same time?

"Jerry!" Stormy screamed and charged toward him, dropping her bunny along the way.

Rayne stooped down and picked up the stuff animal that was nearing its last days. One of its ears and the once fluffy tail, were barely hanging on. She stood back and watched Stormy and Jerry. Each time she saw him, she freaked out. Behaving like he was Santa Claus personally delivering her wished upon present on Christmas morning. Like usual, Jerry scooped her up and gave her a noisy kiss on the cheek.

"How's my ladybug?" he crooned the nickname he'd given her.

Rayne's heart melted a little each time she saw the two of them together. Her daughter giggled, wiggling in his arms as he placed kisses all over her face. This was how she wanted to see Stormy. Happy.

That's all Rayne wanted—for her daughter to be happy...and safe. She tried shielding Stormy from the dramas of their lives, but there were times when she had failed them. Times that Rayne wished she could erase. Like when they had to live in her car for a couple of months. Or like when they had to stay in a seedy hotel because her husband died and left her practically penniless.

Rayne rubbed her chest and stared down at the ground, slowly releasing the breath she hadn't realized she was holding. There had definitely been some dark times in her life

Then one day she ran into her high school friend, Charlee, who was visiting from Cincinnati. After that encounter, one conversation led to another, and Rayne and Stormy had eventually ended up relocating to Cincinnati.

"And I'm going to a new school," Stormy said, pulling Rayne back to the present.

If Jerry hadn't looked so genuinely interested in her daughter's conversation, Rayne would've cut it off. But like usual when dealing with Stormy, he acted like he had no place he needed to be. He listened as if she was explaining the solution to world peace. Rayne had always wanted her daughter to have a positive male role model in her life, and over the last six months, Jerry was turning out to be just that.

Since they'd moved into the neighborhood, he had gone beyond the call of duty to help them. Everything from carrying in groceries, changing a flat tire, and had even come through for her when Mrs. Addy was babysitting, but had a family emergency. That day, Jerry had looked after Stormy until Rayne was able to get home. Before moving to Cincinnati, she didn't have many people she could depend on, but now, she could count on her friend Charlee...and Jerry.

Despite Stormy's incessant conversation, Jerry's gaze found Rayne's. Heat traveled through her body when his eyes did a slow sweep of her body from head to toe. Her nipples pebbled when his eyes stalled on her double D's. She heard that he had a thing for full-figured women, and if his appreciative gaze was any indication, he liked what he saw. She'd been trying to lose thirty pounds since Stormy was a baby, but lately she'd had more pressing issues. Maybe it was time she just embraced her size fourteen.

When Jerry diverted his attention back to Stormy, Rayne took in his appearance. She admired the way his tan T-shirt stretched across his wide chest and broad shoulders. The man didn't have a lick of fat on him and his flat abs were a testament to his daily workouts. Worn, dark jeans sheathed his thick thighs and long legs, while a pair of tan Timberland boots covered his large feet.

She had always been attracted to big, tall, dark skinned men who weren't afraid to get their hands dirty. Jerry fit the bill. Well over six feet tall, he was an electrician and worked for Jenkins & Sons Construction, his family's company. A company that was well-known all over the state of Ohio. At least that's what her friend Charlee had told her when she found out Rayne lived next door to Jerry.

Charlee had also filled her in on his love for women. He'd asked Rayne out more times than she could count, but the last thing she needed was to get involved with another player.

Been there, done that.

Her husband had been a man whore. Too bad she hadn't known that before she married the good-looking, charming bastard and got pregnant. A couple of years after they were married, Kirk had changed. Or maybe he hadn't changed. Maybe she had only seen what she'd wanted to see prior to saying *I do*.

So many mistakes.

Rayne had made one bad decision after another and most centered around Kirk. But in the end, he had gotten what was coming to him, but that left her to clean up his mess.

Feeling her spirits dropping, Rayne stood straighter and pulled her shoulders back. She had come too far in life to let old memories get her down. The move to Cincinnati was a new chapter in her life, and she planned to make the most of it.

I've got this.

Chapter Three

Jerry kept stealing glances at Rayne, noting her off and on troubled expressions. Whatever battle was warring in her head, clearly had her emotions all over the place. Something was definitely bothering her, but what?

"And you know what else?" Stormy asked him, finally stopping her running monologue about a cartoon she'd been watching earlier. His little chatterbox was on a roll today.

"No, what else?"

"I saw Ms. Addy walking down the street with Kari and Rachel," she said of the neighbor who lived on the other side of Rayne. Adeline Mulkie, a retired school teacher, had two granddaughters who were close to Stormy's age. She often watched Stormy on those days when school was closed.

Jerry continued listening as Stormy told him about a book she'd read. God, he loved this little girl. From the moment he met her and she smiled at him, he'd been a goner. A cutie-pie to the nth degree, she was a sweetheart and always smelled like baby powder. But it was her smarts that really caught Jerry's attention, discussing topics that should've exceeded a five-year-old's knowledge. Not many days went by that he didn't see or talk to her.

Stormy was the daughter he wished he had. That was saying a lot for a man who hadn't planned to ever get married, let alone have children. Now that he'd spent time with these two, he could actually picture himself as a family man.

He glanced at Rayne again. At around 5'9, she was tall, thick and curvy just the way he liked. A couple of cousins gravitated toward slim women, but not Jerry. He was a big guy who preferred something to hold onto when it came to holding and loving on a woman.

But with Rayne, more than just her physical makeup turned him on. The woman was downright gorgeous with blemished free reddish-brown skin, long, thick hair, and tempting full lips that were perfect for kissing. Add those features to her wickedly smart brain and beautiful spirit, and she was the perfect catch.

Jerry took in her attire. Normally on the weekends, she wore oversize T-shirts and baggy pants, anything that hid her luscious curves. Not today though. Today she showed off her voluptuous body sporting a fitted V-neck T-shirt that forced his gaze to her full breasts, and jeans that molded over her rounded hips.

Jerry's eyes met hers and a blush painted her cheeks when she realized he was checking her out, much like when he'd caught her checking him out moments ago. He hated that she was fighting their attraction to each other.

"Are you listening?" Stormy asked close to his ear and Jerry stifled a laugh.

"Yeah, I'm listening, baby. So, you're going to the library, huh?"

She nodded, her two ponytails brushing back and forth over her shoulders.

"I almost forgot. Did you get the results back from the test?" Rayne asked Jerry. Months earlier, during one of their conversations, he had mentioned to her that becoming a master electrician would improve his chances of moving up in the company. When the time came to prepare for the exam, Rayne quizzed him on the material, and didn't complain when sessions went late into the night.

"I aced it thanks to you."

For the first time since they'd been standing outside, she smiled. "Oh please. You knew that stuff. You didn't need me."

"Yeah, actually I did. Your encouragement and support got me through those weeks of studying."

"Well...I'm really proud of you."

Her heart-felt words stabbed him in the center of his chest, and if Jerry hadn't been crazy about her before, those words sealed it for him. Despite whatever she was currently going through, she still managed to make him feel special by asking about something that was important to him.

"Thank you. That means a lot."

They stood staring at each other for the longest until Stormy placed her little hands on each side of his face. Her light brown eyes, identical to her mothers, glittered with excitement. "Guess what?"

He laughed at the way she held firm to him, almost bringing them nose to nose while she stared into his eyes. "What?"

"Yesterday was the last day of school, and I was the line leader in my class because I got three gold stars."

"Really?"

She nodded again, her body bursting with excitement. Before he and Rayne started talking about the exam, Stormy had jumped from one topic to the other, but he treasured these moments. This little girl was like a ball of sunshine, brightening his day.

"Can you take me to the human siety?" she asked.

Jerry frowned and glanced at Rayne who stood a couple of feet away. She gave a slight shrug, looking as confused as him.

"The what?" Jerry questioned.

"The human siety. I want to get a puppy."

"Ohhh, the humane society?"

She bobbed her head. "That's what I said."

17

Sharon C. Cooper

"What did I tell you, Stormy?" Rayne interrupted, that stern tone that only mothers could unleash crackling all around them.

With eyes down cast, Stormy sighed and laid her head on Jerry's shoulder, her arms sliding around his neck. He didn't know how Rayne said no to anything this kid wanted. He fell for her cuteness at every turn.

Rayne folded her arms across her chest, her mouth in a thin line while the stuffed bunny dangled from her fingers. "What did I tell you about getting a dog?"

After a long hesitation, Stormy lifted her head and spoke. "You said that you can barely feed me."

Jerry chuckled when Rayne's perfectly arched brows dipped into a frown.

"What else did I tell you?"

"That I had to wait until I was big."

"I told you that when you're old enough to take care of a dog, then I'd think about it. Now come on. I'm sure Jerry has better things to do than hang out here with us."

He glanced at his watch, remembering he needed to drop some paperwork off at work. "I'd rather hang out with my two favorite women, but I do need to make a couple of runs. How about if I cook dinner for us tonight. What do you say?" he asked Rayne.

Even though she wouldn't go on a date with him, the three of them had shared a few meals together over the last couple months. She had cooked twice, and once he'd been able to show off his cooking skills. With their various interactions, they got along great, but she still refused to let their relationship go any further than friendship.

"Can't tonight. I picked up an extra shift at work," she said and strolled across the small patch of grass that separated their driveways.

Unable to help himself, Jerry admired the way her jeans hugged her fine ass as he walked slowly behind her. Sometimes he wondered if Rayne even knew how tempting she was with her beautiful face, enticing body and a toughness about her that made him curious about her past.

She pointed the key fob at the car and unlocked the doors of the old Chevy parked in the driveway. "And Stormy will be at Mrs. Addy's house."

Stormy whined. "But I don't want to. I want to eat with Jerry."

"Tell you what," Jerry said when he got closer to the vehicle, "I'll only be out a few hours. When I get home, I'll whip up a quick meal for all of us before you have to head to work."

Rayne had started to walk around to the other side of the car but stopped near the bumper. "Yeah right. *You're* going to be at home on a Saturday evening…to cook for us?"

She had good reason to be surprised. Normally, he wasn't home much on the weekend, especially for the last few months. Since he'd been keeping a low profile and not hanging out at some of the hot spots where he used to pick up women, he spent more time at some of his cousins' homes. Playing cards, watching sports and movies with them had become a big part of his weekends.

"I'll be here."

Rayne turned to him. "All right, but call if you get tied up."

"All right." He kissed a grinning Stormy on the cheek.

"Do you want a puppy?" Stormy whispered in his ear and Jerry burst out laughing. This kid was persistent if nothing else. Jerry didn't know when, or how, but he'd talk Rayne into getting her a puppy. Or maybe he'd get one himself and let Stormy take care of it. Either way, Rayne would have a fit and they'd both be in the dog house.

A smile lifted the corners of his mouth. "We'll talk about it later," he whispered and Stormy beamed as he put her in her booster seat. He handed her the stuffed bunny before closing the door, then walked around to the other side of the vehicle. He caught Rayne before she climbed into the driver's seat.

"Wait. Close the door for a minute," he said. She looked at him through narrowed eyes but did as he'd asked. "What's wrong?"

She glanced down at her hand, fiddling with her keys. "What do you mean?"

He lifted her chin with the pad of his finger, forcing her to look at him. "I think you know what I mean. Somethin's bothering you, and for the first time since we've known each other, I don't think it's me," he joked.

That got a smile out of her and Jerry zoned in on her mouth, her enticing mouth. God, he wanted to kiss her, but he wouldn't. At least not yet. Not only was Stormy probably watching them, but he was serious about getting to know Rayne better. He didn't want to do anything that would jeopardize the progress he was making.

He lowered his hand from her chin and moved it to her waist, pulling her a little closer. She didn't protest, which reinforced what he was thinking. She wasn't herself today. Whatever was bothering her had stifled the fight that she usually used to brush him and his advances off. As a matter of fact, she'd been the same when he saw her the other day.

"Talk to me. You doing okay?" he asked in a low voice.

Rayne gave a slight nod. "Just a rough couple of days, but I'm fine. Thanks for asking."

"Of course. We're friends, right?"

She nodded again.

"Then what can I do to make you feel better?" Jerry hadn't meant the question to sound suggestive, but the way she huffed out a breath and rolled her eyes meant that he'd done just that.

She pulled out of his grasp. "Bye, Jerry."

"Wait." He grabbed her elbow, stopping her from climbing into the car. Like usual, a high-voltage jolt shot through him as his hand connected with her skin. It didn't help that the coconut scent of her hair wafted by his nose.

"That wasn't a line," he hurried to say. "I'm serious. You look a little down, and I'm concerned. Nothing else." He lifted his hands in surrender, hoping she could see his sincerity. In the few months that they'd gotten to know each other, he considered her a friend. Like any of his other friends or family, if they were troubled, he'd want to do what he could to help.

Her shoulders sagged, and she looked everywhere but at him. "It's nothing I can't handle, but thanks for asking. I better get going."

Jerry opened the door and she climbed into the driver's seat. "All right, but I hope you know you can talk to me about anything."

"Bye, Jerry," Stormy said in a sing-song voice, waving.

"See you later, Ladybug. Be good for mommy."

"Okay," she said.

Jerry positioned his body between the car door and Rayne, one arm resting on the door frame, the other on the roof of the car. "I'll check on you later, all right?"

"Jerry, that's not nec—"

"Just say okay."

That beautiful smile that he didn't see often enough spread across her mouth. "Geesh. Pushy much?"

He grinned. "Maybe a little, but I think you like that about me."

"Whatever." She rolled her eyes, but was still smiling.

"By the way, you look real nice today."

Another blush tinted her cheeks and Jerry winked at her before closing the door. He stepped back, but when Rayne tried to start the car, the engine didn't turn over. She tried again and it still didn't start. Through the window, he didn't miss her frustration, especially when she laid her forehead on the steering wheel.

He knocked on the window, and she lifted her head.

"Popped the hood," he said after she opened the door.

For the next twenty minutes, Jerry tinkered under the hood of the vehicle and had even pulled his truck alongside of hers to give the car a jump, but nothing. He had hoped it was the battery, but he suspected it was either the starter or the alternator, which meant a bigger expense.

"Is our car broke?" Stormy asked. She and Rayne had been standing close by watching his every move.

"I'm afraid so." Jerry closed the hood. "I'll call my mechanic and see if he can pick the car up this afternoon. In the meantime—"

"I..." Rayne shook her head, looking on the verge of tears. "I can't handle another repair expense right now. I'm going to have to—"

"You need a car. A working car. Let's at least see what the problem is and go from there."

He already knew Rayne wouldn't want to accept his help, and he admired her independence. But he was going to help whether she liked it or not. Besides, his mechanic owed him a favor.

Instead of telling her all of that, and dealing with a possible argument, he said, "As for your trip to the library and anywhere else you have to go today, I'll take you. And if we can't get the car fixed before you go to work later, I'll drop you off and pick you up."

Again, she shook her head. "No. I can't ask you to do that. We've imposed on you enough for today. The running around I had planned to do can wait, and I'll figure something out for work."

"We're not going to the library?" Stormy asked on a whine.

"Rayne, it's not a problem. I'm off today. If you don't mind me making a couple of quick stops first, then I'm yours for the rest of the day. Come on. It'll be fun for all of us to hang out."

After a long hesitation, she finally agreed. Jerry felt like doing a fist pump in the air. She'd been trying so hard to keep distance between them, despite the obvious attraction. When all he wanted to do was get to know her better.

"Okay," she finally said. "But if you want to do your running around and then come back and—"

"Nope. We can all leave together. Just let me check my mail, which was why I had originally come out here, and then we can head out."

Stormy jumped up and down. "I'm so excited," she squealed as if he'd told her that he was taking her to Disney World.

Now, if I could just get her mother to be as excited.

Chapter Four

Rayne couldn't remember the last time she had smiled so much. Throughout the morning, they'd bounced from one store to another, taking care of her errands as well as Jerry's. Now they were finally at the library in the children's section.

She looked on as Stormy read Candice Ransom's *Snow Day* to Jerry. Throughout the day, Rayne found herself stealing glances at him. The three of them had spent time together before, mostly at one of their homes, but today felt different. They had moved around the city like a family and it felt so natural. Anyone looking on would've just assumed they were much more than they really were.

Rayne wasn't delusional in thinking that their time together was more than it was—just neighbors...or maybe even friends hanging out. But she couldn't deny that the lightness she currently felt had a lot to do with Jerry. He might be known as a lady's man, but whenever they were together, she saw a man who was patient, funny and laid back. There was also a calmness about him. A calmness that brought out a level of peace within her. Rayne couldn't quite explain it, but she liked the feeling.

"The end," Stormy said, closing the book. "Did you enjoy the story?" she asked, sounding much like the librarian who had just read a book to her and a small group of children.

"I loved it. I knew you were smart, Ladybug, but I didn't know you could read like that," he said and glanced at Rayne.

"Yeah, she's getting better and better. *Snow Day* is a little easy for her, though, but one of her favorite books. I've been working with her on stories that are a little more challenging, but she's a really good reader."

"I can see that," he said, reaching into his pocket for his cell phone that was vibrating in his hand. Glancing at the screen, he stood. "I need to take this. It's Nick and this might have something to do with the paperwork I dropped off," he said of his cousin who oversaw Jenkins & Sons Construction. "I'll be back in a few."

"Can I go?" Stormy asked.

"No," Rayne said as Jerry headed for the exit. "But you can go and pick out three more books before we leave."

"Oh, there's Marlee. Can I go say hi?" Stormy pointed to one of her classmates standing near a rack of books a few feet away.

"Yes, but make sure you stay where I can see you."

Rayne looked down at the stack of books she had already picked out for herself. She had just flipped one open when she felt someone behind her. Glancing over her shoulder, she spotted a familiar face.

"Hey, Rayne. I thought that was you. It's been a while."

"Hi...Calvin," she said, temporarily forgetting the man's name before it popped into her head. Without waiting for an invitation, he sat in the chair that Jerry had vacated.

Rayne had first met Calvin and his young son a few months ago at the library. Last month, they had also run into each other at the grocery store, which was when he had asked her on a date. With each run-in at the library, it had been refreshing to talk to someone who understood how hard it was to juggle work, cooking, shopping and kids' activities as a single parent.

But despite their easy conversations, Rayne wasn't interested in anything more with him. She felt nothing. No real attraction that would make her want to get to know him better. No romantic connection. Besides that, she wasn't ready to start dating. At least not until she got a better handle on her personal life and not until Stormy was older.

"It's good seeing you." Calvin's deep voice was a cross between Barry White and James Earl Jones. Handsome in that smart, nerdy kind of way, including glasses, he looked to be in his mid-thirties with smooth brown skin, expressive eyes beneath bushy brows and a friendly smile that made a person feel immediately at ease. "So how have you been?"

"I've been well, and you?"

"Not bad. Had a little scare with Jr. last week." He nodded toward the little eight-year-old who was near a children's comic book rack. He was a carbon copy of his father, including the glasses.

"What happened last week?"

"He decided it would be a good idea to climb up on the porch railing and then jump off. His foot slipped, and he ended up falling, landing on his arm. Hence the cast he's wearing."

"Oh, no. That had to be scary for you."

"For a while there, yes. Now he's walking around like wearing a cast is the coolest thing ever, especially with all the attention he's been getting from everyone he meets."

Rayne shook her head smiling. "*Kids*. They freak us out with their stunts, then move on before our heart rates get back to normal."

"Tell me about it." He crossed one leg over the other and nodded toward her opened book. "What are you reading?"

Rayne lifted the book, showing him the cover. "*Becoming*, by Michelle Obama. I just got it a few minutes ago. The library had a long waiting list for it, but I guess they purchased additional copies. So it came in sooner than I expected."

"Yeah, it's on my TBR list. You'll have to tell me what you thought about it once you're done."

"Did you ever finish Zig Ziglar's, *Embrace the Struggle?*"

Ziglar had been one of Rayne's favorite motivational speakers and she'd read most of his work, especially during some of her most trying years after Kirk's death.

"I did. I'm glad you recommended it. It was a good read. Inspiring. I even picked up some of his older work."

She kept an eye on Stormy while her and Calvin's conversation bounced from books to weather and even to the NBA finals. Most guys were surprised by her knowledge of basketball, most she picked up as a kid. While married, Rayne had watched the sport in an effort to bond with Kirk. Lotta good that did, though. It still hadn't been enough to make him want to spend more time at home or with her.

On the other hand, being a fan of the game had its benefits. Watching basketball was a great source of entertainment during the winter, and it was also one of many things she and Jerry had in common. There had been a few times after Stormy was put to bed that they'd watch a game or two together. Knowing how much she enjoyed the sport, he had often invited her to watch him and some of his cousins play. They played every other Sunday morning, but she usually found an excuse of why she couldn't attend, even when she'd been tempted to go.

That thought made her think about how often he invited her places. Normally, her response was always no, but lately it was getting harder to say no to him. She enjoyed his company and wondered...

Rayne glanced down at the book in her hand as Calvin gave her a play by play of last night's Lakers game. How crazy was it that she was sitting there with a nice, good-looking guy, but thinking about Jerry? She knew it wasn't just because he was at the library. With the few encounters she'd had with other men since the move, she tended to compare them to Jerry.

Stormy came running down the aisle, slamming into Rayne and wrapping her arm around her waist. With Rayne sitting down, that almost brought them face to face.

"Mommy, is Jerry playing basketball before he cooks?"

Rayne stared at her daughter. Sometimes this kid scared her. Jerry hadn't said anything about playing basketball. So she wasn't sure where Stormy got that idea. What was spookier, Rayne had just been thinking about him…and basketball.

There were moments, like right now, it felt as if Stormy could somehow sense whatever Rayne was feeling or thinking. This happened too often to be a coincident. Yes, they had a special connection as mother and daughter, but could it be that strong?

"Who's Jerry?" Calvin asked.

"My friend," Stormy volunteered. "He's going to cook dinner for us."

Calvin's eyes met Rayne's. "I see."

"Actually, it's probably time we got going. Stormy, where are the books you picked out?" Rayne stacked her own books while her daughter took off, probably to quickly pick out books that she should've had already. "Calvin, it was good talking to you. I'm sure we'll see you here again sometime."

"Or, you can finally accept my invitation to go out to dinner one evening."

"That's not going to happen. She's not available."

Rayne whirled around at the sound of Jerry's voice. Shocked at the coldness in his tone, as well as his words. The icy glare in his eyes kept her from saying anything, though. He moved closer to her side and Rayne could feel the tension bouncing off of him.

"Jerry!" Stormy ran toward them with books under her arm.

"Shush, you're in the library," Rayne whispered.

"Sorry," Stormy mumbled then lifted her arms to Jerry, who automatically picked her up, books and all.

"You must be the cook," Calvin said, a smirk on his face when he looked at Jerry. "Stormy was just saying th—"

"He's not a cook," Stormy interrupted defensively, to Rayne's surprise. "He's an electrician. I'm going to be one too when I get big."

Okay, what is happening here?

"Actually, Calvin, this is Jerry Jenkins," Rayne jumped in, afraid of what else Stormy might share. "And Jerry, this is Calvin…" His last name slipped her mind.

"Butler. Calvin Butler," Calvin said. He extended his hand, and Jerry was slow to accept it, but eventually did, holding on a little longer than Rayne thought necessary. And she was pretty sure there was some silent communication going on between the men considering the way they glared at each other.

"Well, I'd better go and check on my son," Calvin said when they dropped hands. "It was good seeing you again, Rayne." He nodded at Jerry and left them standing there.

"What was that all about?" Rayne asked.

"You two ready to go?" he asked instead of answering her question, and he glanced at Stormy who was looking between them. The tension Rayne felt from him moments ago was still present.

She sighed, thinking a library probably wasn't the best place to have the conversation they clearly needed to have, especially with Stormy right there.

"Yeah, I'm ready to go," she finally said.

A short while later they were leaving the library's parking lot, and Jerry still hadn't spoken.

"What was that all about back there?" Rayne asked only loud enough for him to hear. Stormy wasn't paying them any attention since Jerry had let her use his cell phone to play a game.

"Not now, Rayne."

Part of her wanted to snap at him, not missing the edge in his voice as he maneuvered the truck through the streets of

Cincinnati. But the smart part of her, the part that didn't want to argue in front of her daughter, kept quiet.

"Can we get some ice cream now?" Stormy asked.

Crap. Rayne had forgotten about getting ice cream before going home. But considering Jerry's funky attitude, maybe today wasn't a good...

"Sounds good to me." Jerry glanced at Rayne as if to ask if she was okay with that. "I'm thinking it shouldn't ruin her appetite for dinner since we won't be eating for another few hours."

"So dinner is still on?"

Jerry, splitting his attention between her and the road, frowned at her. "Why wouldn't it be?"

Rayne shrugged. "Oh, I don't know. Maybe because you've been acting funny since we left the library. What was—"

"Mommy, what did Jerry say funny?" Stormy asked from the back seat.

So much for talking quietly.

Rayne shook her head, and Jerry's lips twitched, trying to keep from laughing. If nothing else, the question got him to loosen up.

"He didn't say anything funny, honey."

"But you said—"

"Ladybug, what type of ice cream are you getting when we get to Graeter's?" Jerry asked.

"Strawberry. And I'm going to get some chocolate on it and some..."

Rayne glanced at Jerry as Stormy went on and on about ice cream, changing her mind every few seconds about what she planned to get.

"Thank you," Rayne mouthed to Jerry. She'd been raising Stormy on her own for years, but she had to admit that it was nice having someone to tag team with, even if only for the day.

*

30

Jerry and Rayne strolled across the ice cream parlor to a table in the corner. He pulled out a chair for her and glanced to his left. Moments after they walked in, Stormy had made a couple of friends. Now the three of them claimed a small table nearby and it sounded like they were discussing what type of ice cream they should've gotten.

Jerry sat next to Rayne. He swiped his tongue over the ice cream, lapping up a nice amount of rocky road from his cone.

"When did you start volunteering at the women's shelter?" he asked. One of their stops earlier had been to Cincinnati Refuge for Women so Rayne could drop off a box of donations.

"A little more than a month ago. One of my co-workers set up a box in the women's locker room at work for donations, mainly toiletries for homeless women and children. Anyway, she had to take a temporary leave of absence and asked for volunteers to drop off the items whenever the box got full. I offered to make the delivery. When I went to the facility and talked with the director, I was moved by all that they were doing. Then I decided to volunteer a couple of hours on Sundays and help tutor women who are trying to get their GED."

Jerry nodded, even more impressed with her. It took a special person to give up what little free time they had to help someone else. "That's cool. Why didn't you ever say anything?"

She gave a slight shrug. "I don't know. I guess the topic never came up."

"Did you do volunteer work in San Antonio?"

Even though Rayne rarely talked about herself, occasionally she'd say something that gave him a little insight into her past.

"In my senior year of high school, I volunteered at a food pantry. After I got married, though, I stopped. But when I was homeless a while back..."

Whoa. Wait. What?

She kept talking, but Jerry wanted to stop her right there. Instead, he kept quiet, hoping she'd explain.

"I had vowed to start back volunteering once I was able," she continued as if she hadn't just dropped a bomb. "I know how easy it is to hit rock bottom and not know where your next meal is coming from. So now I try to give back anyway I can."

When she didn't give details about being homeless, he asked, "How'd you end up homeless?"

Seconds ticked by without her responding and just when he thought she wouldn't answer the question, Rayne said, "It's a long story. I rather not talk about it right now."

She glanced at the table where Stormy was giggling with her new friends. Jerry wanted so bad to press Rayne for more information, but she was right, that wasn't the best place to have a serious conversation. Each time she shared a little bit of her past, he was left with more questions that he intended to one day get answers to.

"Your choice surprises me." He nodded at her single scoop of vanilla ice cream. "You passed on orange cream, butter pecan, and didn't even get a waffle cone. What's that all about? We come to the best ice cream parlor in the country, and you order...*vanilla*," he said with playful disdain. "You don't strike me as a vanilla type of person."

She actually struck him more as a cookies and cream, or a decadent strawberry chocolate chip type of person. There was a fun, vibrancy about her that she kept under wraps and only let slip out on occasion. As if she had to always be straight-laced and serious, not wanting anyone to know that she had a fun and free side to her.

Jerry didn't know for sure if that was the case, but he had a feeling Rayne wasn't as innocent...or vanilla as she let on. If only she would let him in a little, maybe he could bring the real her to life.

With the plastic spoon, she scooped up a small amount of ice cream from the cup and brought it to her lips. Her perfectly shaped...kissable lips. He watched as she glided the spoon into her mouth, her eyes fluttering as she savored the icy treat. Even the way she slowly slid the spoon out was a turn on. How could such a simple gesture look so sensual?

Her tongue slid out and she licked the spoon. "I'm keeping sweets to a minimum since I'm trying to drop a few pounds."

That snapped Jerry out of his trance. "Why?"

Her brows dipped into a frown when she looked at him. "What do you mean, why? Look at me."

"Baby, I am looking at you, and I love what I see."

She gave an unladylike snort and stuck her spoon back into the cup for another scoop of ice cream. "I'm not sure what you see, but I doubt you usually hang out with women who don't spend much time in the gym like you do. Or those who look at food and gain ten pounds. Or anyone who's wardrobe only consists of big, baggy shirts and stretch pants."

Frustration drummed through his veins. "I hate when you do that."

"When I do what?"

"When you put yourself down. Sometimes I wonder if you even know how gorgeous you are. And for the record," he lowered his voice. "You're the perfect size. I'm a big guy. What the hell am I going to do with some skinny chick? I prefer a woman with meat on her bones."

"I—I didn't realize I was putting myself down. I was...I was just stating fact."

"Well, the fact is, I like you, Rayne, just the way you are, inside and out. And I'm hoping to get to know you even better."

She shook her head and chuckled. "Jerry, I like you too, more than you know, but we've had this conversation. I'm not dating you."

"Why, because you're interested in Calvin?"

Jerry had never been the jealous type when it came to the women he dated, but none of those women had been Rayne. When he heard Calvin ask her out, he wanted to throat punch the guy.

"I'm not in…wait. Is that why you were rude at the library?"

"I wasn't rude. I just didn't appreciate him trying to move in on my territory."

"What territory? You and I are just friends."

"With the potential of being *so* much more." He winked. "Besides, you couldn't date that guy even if you wanted to."

Her spoon stopped mid-way to her mouth, and she frowned. "Excuse me? What gives you the right to say who I can or can't date?"

He held up his free hand and kept his voice low. "Hey, it's not me. It's Stormy."

Rayne glanced at her daughter before moving closer to Jerry and leaning in. The coconut scent of her hair even more pronounced, making him want to pull her closer.

"Did she say something to you?" she asked in a whisper.

Jerry licked his ice cream, catching some of the melting, sweet treat with his tongue before it started down the side of the waffle cone.

"She didn't have to say anything. I'm a little surprised that you didn't notice."

"Notice what?"

"How she treated ol' boy." He kept his voice low. "Ladybug likes everyone. She's always smiling, striking up conversation, and asking people their name, but she had a different vibe with your friend."

"He's not my friend," Rayne said defensively, looking deep in thought as she sat back in her seat.

Jerry was pretty sure she wasn't interested in Calvin. Otherwise, Stormy's reaction would've jumped out to her. She also probably would've addressed her daughter's tone at the way she practically snapped at the man.

"I'm assuming you're not interested in him."

"Right now, I'm only interested in raising my daughter. Dating is not a part of my plans."

"It could be. You can date *me* and still take care of Ladybug. You know I would never do anything to come between you and her."

"I know. It's just that I don't think I'm ready to start dating yet."

Jerry nodded. "Okay, but just as a heads up, I might ask you out again."

She laughed. "Well, thanks for the warning. I'll get my *'no'* all ready for you."

Jerry grinned at her. Except for the run in with the Calvin guy, the day had been perfect. They fit together well, even if Rayne was still trying to keep him at a distance.

But little did she know, he was a patient man who always went after what he wanted. And he wanted Rayne Ellison.

Chapter Five

"You're not ready."

Jerry glared at Nick, his hands balled into a fist at his sides, itching to punch his cousin in the mouth. As the big boss, Nick might have the final say in all things pertaining to the family business, but he was wrong in this case. Jerry was perfect for the electrician foreman's position. Granted he'd have to wait a couple of months for Ted, the current foreman, to retire, but he was ready.

Nick removed his reading glasses and set them on the desk. In his mid-thirties, they were about the same in height and weight, but his cousin was a few years older. The good Jenkins' genes that much of the family bragged about had spilled onto Nick, making him look at least ten years younger than his actual age.

"I need someone dependable, quick on their feet, and a person who can lead a team of twenty-five people. I'll admit, your electrical skills and your ability to appease customers when a job isn't going quite right, is on point. But Jay, there is so much more to the job."

Jerry placed his hands, palms down, on top of Nick's desk. "I'm the best damn electrician here and you know it."

"That might be so, but that doesn't mean you're qualified to run that department." Nick leaned back and rocked in his high-back, leather desk chair, rubbing the scruff on his chin. "I need someone I can trust to use good judgment."

"I can do—"

"Someone who shows up to jobs and meetings on time," Nick continued. "Someone who maintains a professional image while on the job and when he *or she* is off duty. But my number one concern with you is how you interact with our female clientele."

"What? Did someone complain about me?"

"On the contrary. They love you, but in my opinion, you're a little too…friendly at times."

"*Really*, Nick? That's what you're concerned about? You harp on us always providing a good customer experience. Yet, you're trying to tell me that—"

"I don't ever want a situation to arise that someone misinterprets your good intentions. As head of a department, you're not only dealing with customers but also vendors and employees. Though we haven't had to deal with this, claims of sexual misconduct or assault, as well as harassment is real. In this climate, we can never be too careful. And your *friendliness* could easily be mistaken for more than you intend. If you know what I mean."

Yeah, Jerry knew what he meant. He flirted. Sometimes a little too much. Other times he didn't even realize he was doing it. Either way, it was never with the intention of stepping over any moral lines or to make anyone uncomfortable. But he could see where that behavior could be a problem.

He straightened and shoved his hands into the front pockets of his jeans. "Well, my days of flirting are over." For more reasons than one, he started to say, but instead said, "I want this position."

Nick studied him for the longest time in that way that would make a weaker man look away. Jerry met his gaze. He had seen the look plenty of times. It was similar to the intense look their grandfather, Steven Jenkins, the patriarch of the family had perfected when talking to a business associate. Or when he was dealing with Jerry or one of the cousins who did something to embarrass the family.

"Why do you want the position?" Nick asked.

Jerry dropped down into one of the chairs sitting in front of the desk. "Because I'm ready for more responsibility. I know the business and the company's values and policies better than anyone in that department. I can be a good leader if given the chance."

Nick shook his head. "I don't know, dude. You've done some shady shit over the years...on company time."

"Man, I was a kid. I'm older and wiser now."

He'd started working around the shop while in high school and then went through the electrical apprenticeship right after graduation. Jerry couldn't count the number of times his sister, Peyton, who used to run the company, had threatened to fire him for one stupid stunt or another.

"Besides, I didn't do anything that couldn't be corrected."

"Yeah, ninety-nine percent of the time the situations worked out, but now you're asking me to put you in charge of a department. That involves me trusting that you won't do something crazy to screw up the whole company. It also involves tons of paperwork, hiring, firing, and sometimes long hours."

"I'm telling you, Nick, I can do it."

Before Nick could respond, a knock on the door snagged their attention before it swung open.

"Nick, what do you want to do about," Martina Jenkins-Kendricks, started but stopped when she realized Jerry was in the office. "Oops, sorry. I didn't realize you guys were still meeting."

Jerry didn't know what was going on with his cousin, who they referred to as MJ. Lately, she'd been more considerate, more chill, and...basically not herself. He could attribute it to marrying Paul, a former U.S. senator, but they'd been married a few years now. This behavior was new.

She looked the same, with her customary baseball cap pulled low over her eyes, but the vibe she was giving off seemed more mellow than usual. Most days, she was that loud-mouth, pain-in-the-butt family member that every family had at least one of. Any other time she wouldn't have apologize for barging in. She would've plopped down in a seat and started prying into whatever they were discussing, but not this morning. Today she seemed almost...human.

Maybe she was changing, too.

Internally Jerry chuckled at the thought because he couldn't imagine her any other way than the pain in the ass that she usually was with the family. Yet, if he could change his ways and become the upstanding man he desired to be, why was it hard to believe that she couldn't change?

"What's up?" Nick asked her. Martina was a carpenter by trade, and second in command at J & S.

"Nothing too major. The Listermans decided they didn't want to go with the maple hardwood flooring we purchased. They liked it but prefer to go with something a little lighter. Lucky for them, Volenski wants the hardwood for his place. I'll just have to order a little more."

Nick sat forward. "So, what's the problem?"

"Do you want to charge the Listermans the restocking and inconvenience fee?"

"We can let it slide this time, unless they decide to change something else that we've already ordered."

"That works for me." She headed to the door.

"Wait," Jerry called out. "Before you leave, can you weigh in on a debate that Nick and I are having?"

"Let me guess," she put her hand on her hip, her weight mostly on one leg, "this is about the foremen's position that doesn't exist yet. Right?" She smirked, her typical smartass-self peeking through her professional veneer.

"You guessed it," Nick said. "I don't think Jerry's ready for that type of responsibility."

"And I told you that I am," Jerry snapped, banging his fist on the desk. "I'm perfect for the position!" He turned to Martina. "Be honest, MJ. Do you think I can do the job?"

"Yeah, actually, I think you can."

Both Jerry and Nick were struck speechless. Sure, Jerry wanted her to agree with him, he just hadn't expected it to be that easy. What he expected was...

"You might be a big-headed, stupid, jerk with an oversize ego, but you know your way around wires and electrical systems. I hate to say it, but your cocky ass would make a helluva foreman."

Cocky?

"Now, can I get back to work? I don't have time for this shit."

The moment the door closed behind her, Nick burst out laughing.

A growl rumbled inside of Jerry's chest. "I hate her."

"What did you expect?" Nick asked, still chuckling. "She's incapable of saying anything nice about someone without throwing shade. It's against her nature."

So much for thinking she had changed.

Jerry leaned forward, his forearms on the desk. "I'm telling you, Nick, I can do it. I'm ready. All I need is a chance to prove it. Besides, I'm taking a page out of your book."

Nick's brows shot up. "Is that right? How so?"

"I'm...positioning myself."

"For?" He dragged out the word, looking skeptical.

Jerry sat back and rubbed his forehead before meeting Nick's gaze again. "You've probably noticed that over the last few months, I've been snatching up as much overtime as I can get."

"Yeah, and?"

"And besides my townhome, I'm debt free. Outside of my mortgage and keeping a few dollars of spending money in my pocket, I've been saving and investing everything else. I'm not just changing myself, but I'm preparing for when I have a family."

That was one thing that Jerry had admired about Nick. For as long as he'd known his cousin, Nick had been serious about business and saving for the future. His cousin was seven years older, but wiser beyond his years. He used to hang on to almost every penny he made, claiming he wanted to be financially stable before he got married. And he had done just that.

Jerry had heard that as a teenager, Nick had a financial and life plan that he stuck with, until he met his wife, Sumeera. Even then, it had taken losing her before he was willing to tweak his strategy and win her back. Now they were happily married with a little girl and a baby on the way.

Nick stared at him, studying Jerry as if waiting for him to say more, then he burst out laughing again. He rocked in his seat and pounded the top of the desk as his laughter grew louder.

What the hell?

Jerry sat back in his seat and huffed out a breath, waiting for the jerk to calm down. He couldn't be too upset at the blatant disrespect. He was the one who vowed repeatedly to anyone who would listen that he would never settle down with one woman when there were so many to choose from. But now...

"Wait. You're serious?"

"Yeah, asshole. I'm serious. It's a good thing I don't suffer from low self-esteem. Between you, Liam, and MJ, I would have a complex."

"Well...damn, man. You forget, we know how immature you can be."

"Past tense. I'm not that guy anymore."

"So you say."

"Give me a chance to prove that I'm the best person to fill that position."

"All right, but I'm not going to just slide you into that seat. I'll be watching you until we're ready to make a decision. I'm also talking to Ted for some recommendations. Just know that this might be your only shot to prove to me and the family that you're as changed as you claim to be. Now get out of my office. I'm sure the client is probably wondering where you are."

"I already called and told them I'd be late." Jerry lifted his hand when Nick started to speak. "Everything is cool, especially since I told them that the job would be done today."

"Okay, get to it then."

Jerry fist bumped his cousin before heading to the door. Proving to his family that he was a changed man was going to be an uphill battle. But like getting Rayne to give him a chance, he was ready for the challenge.

Chapter Six

Jerry glanced at his watch, the third time in the last thirty minutes. He had a few hours to finish up this job, and what he didn't want to do was be late getting home. When he'd found out Rayne had to work a late shift and was planning to catch the bus, he insisted on dropping her off at work.

She had been without her car for three days and it was starting to wear on her, especially when she found out she needed a new alternator. Jerry still remembered the relief in her beautiful eyes when he'd told her that there wouldn't be a charge for the car repair. He had a feeling money was tighter than she let on.

He was pulled out of his thoughts when the door alarm chimed, signaling someone was entering the house that he was working in. He assumed it was either Mr. or Mrs. Brooks, the owners, returning.

"Mom, you here?" a familiar voice called out.

Jerry finished attaching the twist-on wire connectors to a set of wires before pushing them back into the small opening in the ceiling. The click-clack of high heels on the hardwood floor grew closer to the kitchen and dining room combo where he was working.

"What a pleasant surprise."

Jerry glanced down from the top of the ladder, recognizing the sultry voice of a woman he hadn't seen in almost a year.

"Hey, what's up, girl?" He placed the wire cutters in the side pocket of the tool belt hanging low around his waist and climbed down the ladder. Dana Brooks was the last person he expected to see.

"When my mother told me that she had called in an electrician, I thought of you, but had no idea that you'd be the person to show up."

"I hadn't made the connection that you were related to Mr. & Mrs. Brooks. So how have you been? It's been a long time."

"Yes, it has. Too long." She wrapped her arms around his neck and one of his hands went automatically to her waist as they hugged. Against his will, Jerry inhaled her familiar scent.

Cashmere Mist, a Donna Karan fragrance that he'd once purchased for her. They'd had a good time whenever they *hooked up*, but now, the way her hands trailed down his chest and to his waist felt wrong on so many levels.

But before he could move back, Dana brushed her lips over his, as if she had every right to do so. All types of warning bells sounded through his head. There'd been a time her touch wouldn't have phased him, but now he had too much at stake.

When her fingers went lower and she cupped him, squeezing his package, he sucked in a breath and grabbed hold of her hand. "Don't."

She met his gaze. One perfectly arched brow lifted upward, and surprise sparkled in her eyes. Her mouth twitched. It wasn't quite a smile, but more of an overconfident smirk on her full, red lips.

"Okay, so this is new," she murmured when he stepped back.

This moment was almost comical. Him...uncomfortable? That was unheard of. Rarely, if ever, did he back away from a woman, especially a beautiful one. Dressed in business attire, Dana wore a light-blue blouse with the top two buttons undone. It revealed just enough cleavage that wouldn't be considered indecent in an office, but he knew what lay beneath the thin material. Large breasts.

Beautiful.

Full.

Soft breasts.

He might not be interested in her, but he couldn't deny that she still had the body of a seductress. She was an enticing woman in the tight, straight navy-blue skirt that stopped just above her knees. Her thick, shapely legs and sky-high shoes added to the look. But Jerry had no desire to flirt and charm her the way he would've done any other time.

Today was the first of many days that he was on a mission to ensure that the changes in him could be seen and felt by everyone who knew him well. And Dana knew him well.

"If I didn't know better, I'd think you were shooting down my advances. But I know better." Each step she took forward, he took a step back as if they were practicing a dance routine. "There's no way in hell the Jerry Jenkins I know, the one who would pull a woman into a bathroom stall and fuck her senseless, would turn down all of this," she said, her hands squeezing her large breasts before skimming over her body and stopping at her wide hips.

In his heart, he belonged to another woman, Rayne. But damn if his dick didn't twitch with the way this woman caressed her body. He had seen her naked countless times and watching her now reminded him of her curves, her softness, and her intoxicating scent.

Yet, with those thoughts came thoughts of Rayne. A woman who didn't give a damn that he was crazy about her and refused to give them a chance to get to know each other better. But that didn't stop him from believing she was the one for him.

45

Crazy? Maybe. But Jerry had no intention of messing up any chance he had with her. Besides that, he was in his customers' home. All he needed was for her folks to return while he ravished their daughter's tempting body.

Between his feelings for Rayne, and his impending promotion, he had too much at stake to screw it up for some tail. Tail he'd already had. The thought was like ice water being poured over his head, rolling down his body and freezing every part of him before landing on the floor.

Dana's hands went to the buttons on her blouse, unbuttoning one and then another, revealing a lace bra the same color as her top.

"Come on, Jerry. Quit playin'. We can get in a quickie before my mother returns and before I have to get back to work."

Jerry sidestepped her and glanced at his watch, then pulled his cell phone from his pocket. He wanted to make sure he was still on schedule and could be finished on time. He also wanted some backup.

Not trusting his common sense, he shot a quick text to his cousin Martina, knowing she was working in the area. The discomfort he was currently feeling with Dana's presence and his wayward thoughts were real. But he had too much to lose if he chose wrong in this situation.

Dana had always been easy when it came to him, willing to give him whatever he wanted. With the slightest encouragement, she'd hike up her skirt and drop her panties, assuming she was wearing any, and Jerry had no intention of finding out.

Within seconds, Martina responded to his text.

On my way.

A sigh of relief slipped between his lips and when he looked up, his gaze met Dana's. She stopped moving, her hands on her hips as her eyes narrowed in on him.

"What was that all about?" she asked motioning toward his cell.

Jerry held up the device. "I'm on a time crunch and was checking in with my supervisor."

Now she was glaring. "I'm offering up myself to you and you're texting your boss?"

He shrugged, slipping his phone into the front pocket of his jeans. "Listen, baby. I mean...Dana. I ain't gon' lie. You're still one of the most beautiful women I've ever met." Her expression softened, and she let her arms drop to her sides, a sweet smile covered her ruby red lips. "There are two things going on here. First of all, I'm working. I have to finish this job by a certain time. Secondly, I'm involved with someone." Okay, so that was a little lie, but in reality, his heart belonged to Rayne whether she knew it or not. Nothing was going to change that. Not even fine-ass Dana. "So you and me...ain't gonna happen."

She closed the distance between them. "You being involved with someone never stopped us before."

In the past when he was *involved* with someone, it was just a hook up. One that both parties understood meant nothing.

"You know better than anyone that we were just having a good time."

"That may be true, but that doesn't mean that the women you were with didn't feel like they were the only one in your life. So—"

"None of that matters to me right now. I'm not that guy anymore, Dana." He didn't care that he and Rayne were currently just friends. He believed those words and spoke them with enough conviction that anyone hearing him would believe them.

"That's bullshit," Dana spat.

Okay, maybe not, but that didn't make them any less true.

"You're incapable of being with just one woman, and if this chick you're involved with believes otherwise, she's a damn fool."

47

Anger rolled inside of him. He didn't have to explain himself or his feelings for Rayne to anyone, but right now that's exactly what he wanted to do. But then he thought about what Liam said about showing a woman versus telling them. That went for Rayne and any of the women in his past.

"Me on the other hand," Dana continued. "I understand the type of man you are. You love women, and we love you. You're a freak in bed, capable of bringing a woman pleasure with only a—"

The doorbell rang before Dana could finish and not a moment too soon. The last thing Jerry wanted to hear out of her mouth were details of how he pleasured a woman.

He removed his tool belt and set it on the floor. "That's probably for me." He headed down the long hallway to the front of the house, glad to see Martina on the other side of the glass door. He didn't have to look over his shoulder to know that Dana had followed him. Now he had to figure out how to play this. He never asked Martina to come to his rescue, mainly because she loved giving family members a hard time, especially when they were in a bind.

"Hey, what's up?" he greeted, being sure to make eye contact, hoping she could read his desperation.

"You tell me." She walked in like the badass she was, looking him up and down, probably trying to hold back a smart-ass comment since they had an audience. Her amused gaze took in Dana, who stood a few feet away, before returning to him. "I came to see what was taking you so long on this job. Now I see. Was this job...too much for you?"

Jerry fought back a laugh. "Of course not. I can handle anything thrown my way. This job is just a little...trickier than usual. Wanna come see."

"Lead the way."

They walked down the hallway, slowing when they reached Dana.

"Dana, this is one of my bosses, Martina. MJ, this is Dana, Mr. and Mrs. Brooks daughter and an old friend."

Both women greeted each other with a nod before he and Martina continued to where he was working.

"Hey, um, Jerry," Dana said from behind them. "I'm gonna get going. It was good seeing you. I'll be in touch."

"It was good seeing you again, Dana, but I think we've said all we needed to say."

Instead of acknowledging his words, she smirked again. "Nice meeting you Martina. You two have a good day."

The moment the door closed behind Dana, Martina whirled on him. "What the hell, man? Yo punk-ass called me in here to run a woman away?"

"I was trying to get out of a sticky situation and figured I'd call in reinforcements."

"Yeah, tell it to someone else." She laughed, shaking her head while looking up at the holes in the ceiling where recessed lights were going. "It's been a while since I've had anything on you. Sunday brunch is going to be fun, especially when I tell everyone that you're afraid of women. And why is that?"

Jerry rolled his eyes. "I'm not afraid of anyone."

Each week, the family was expected to show up at his grandparents' estate for Sunday brunch. Their family was close and their grandmother wanted to keep it that way, often saying that a family who eats together, stays together. Most made it a point to be there every week, but whenever any of her grandchildren didn't show, come Monday morning they could expect a call from her.

But no matter what defense Jerry used right now with Martina, it wouldn't matter. She wouldn't believe the truth. Whatever he said, come Sunday, she'd embellish the truth anyway to make her story about him more humiliating. She was good at her ruthlessness. But with that, she was also the first to come to any of their rescue if needed.

Jerry put his tool belt back on and moved the ladder to the next ceiling hole. "You can go now."

"But what if your black widow comes back? Who will save you?"

Jerry chuckled. *And it begins.*

"Can't you just forget that I asked you to come by and run interference?"

"*Hell* no."

"Then can you just leave so I can get this job done before five?"

"I could, but it would be more fun to stick around and pick on—"

"Bye, MJ. Don't let the doorknob hit you where the good Lord—"

"Yeah, yeah, I got it. I'm out, but this isn't over."

"I'm sure."

*

Hours later, Jerry brought his truck to a screeching halt in Rayne's driveway and jumped out. She was going to kill him. She only had twenty minutes to get to work. Not only was he late, but he had waited until the last possible minute to call and let her know that he was on his way.

Before he could knock, Rayne's door swung open. "If I'm late for work, I'm blaming you. Why would you volunteer to drop me off if—"

On impulse, Jerry's arm around went around her waist. He placed a lingering kiss on her soft lips, not surprised by the electrical charge of desire that shot through his body. If an innocent kiss stirred something this wicked inside of him, he could only imagine what it would be like when they finally made love.

He broke off the lip-lock suddenly. Maybe kissing her hadn't been the smartest thing to do, but seeing those angry eyes, did something to Jerry. The need to kiss the worry off her face was stronger than the plan to go slow with her.

"I'm sorry. Not about the kiss but about being late," Jerry said when he released her.

Rayne remained in the doorway staring at him with wide eyes, her fingers hovering near her lips. For a moment neither of them spoke, and Jerry was sure he had just ruined any

50

chance of them getting together. But damn if he didn't want to kiss her again. But he wouldn't, at least not right now.

"Grab your things so we can go. Where's Ladybug?"

After a slight hesitation she said, "I already took her to Mrs. Addy's house. Um…maybe you taking me to work isn't a good idea. I can call a—"

"Rayne? Do you want to stand here arguing with me or get to work on time?"

"But…" She looked unsure then huffed out a breath. "Fine. Let's just go."

Within minutes they were on their way. A couple of miles into the drive and Rayne still hadn't spoken and stared out of the passenger side window. Jerry would rather her chew him out instead of giving him the silent treatment, but what had he expected? He would've been mad too if someone had offered to take him somewhere, actually insisting on it, but then didn't show until late.

Splitting his attention between Rayne and the road, he reached over and covered her hand with his. "Listen, I messed up. I know I promised to be home on time. But I got caught up at work trying to finish a project and lost track of time. I know I should've called you sooner than I did, but I didn't want you to make other arrangements."

Rayne hadn't wanted to impose and had told him that morning that she would find a way to work, but he had insisted on taking her. The more time they spent together, the more time he wanted to spend with her. Besides, he liked having her depend on him. Maybe it was chauvinistic, but it felt good to help her out.

"I hope you know I would never intentionally go back on my word, or make you late for work."

"I know but… When you've been disappointed as much as I've been, it's hard to trust that someone will follow through on a promise."

Damn. Way to make me feel even more like crap.

Jerry squeezed her hand before releasing it. He didn't know everything about her past, but considering how standoffish she'd been when first moving to the neighborhood, he knew she had a story. Each time he asked about her life in San Antonio, where she had lived before moving to Cincinnati, she'd share just enough to make him want to know more. Or she shut down.

Whatever Rayne left behind, or whatever she was running from, had shaken her pretty good. If Jerry ever planned to have a future with her, he couldn't afford to let her down again. He wanted her to trust and depend on him.

Minutes later, he turned into the parking lot of the factory and sped toward the entrance. When she went for the door handle, he stopped her with a hand on her arm.

"Sit tight. I'll get that for you."

Jerry hurried to the passenger side. The truck was taller than most and he extended a hand to help her down. "Ten-thirty, right?" he asked of the time she was scheduled to get off of work.

Rayne nodded, staring at him, then quickly looked away but not before he saw pain in her eyes.

Ah, man. "Hey." He moved closer and put his hand at the back of her neck, forcing her to look at him. "What's wrong? If this is about me being late, I'm sorry, sweetheart. I know I cut it close, but—"

"I know. It's not…" She bit down on her bottom lip, blinking several times. "I'm just… It's just that…besides my friend Charlee and Mrs. Addy, you're the only other person I can depend on and…" She waved away the rest of her statement. "Don't mind me. I'm trippin'. Thanks for dropping me off. Actually, thanks for all you do for me and Stormy. I mean that. I don't say it enough, but I really do appreciate you."

Relief flooded through Jerry. "So does this mean that you'll finally go out to dinner with me?"

"Oh, no. That hasn't changed, especially since you were late." Her words were spoken teasingly.

"All right, but just so that you know, I'm not giving up." Not caring if she tried pushing him away, he pulled her close.

"And for the record, you and Ladybug mean a lot to me. Anything I do for either of you is my pleasure." He placed a kiss on the side of her head and reluctantly released her. "I'll be here when you get off."

Jerry watched as she hurried to the building. She reached the door, but stopped and glanced back. His heart leaped in his chest when she smiled at him before going in.

Shaking his head, he chuckled as he climbed back into his truck. All it took was a smile, and she had his chest sticking out, making him feel like her hero. What would happen when she finally agreed to go out with him?

Chapter Seven

"I'm so happy," Stormy squealed, jumping up and down near the kitchen counter where Rayne was mixing pancake batter.

"You act as if it's your birthday," Rayne said, amused that her daughter was excited about them cooking breakfast for Jerry.

Rayne hadn't seen much of him, not since a week ago when he dropped her off at the repair shop. But since then, he hadn't been far from her mind. Yes, she'd been temporarily ticked at him for almost making her late for work that one day, but that hadn't lasted long. Her heart swelled thinking about how he'd gone beyond the call of duty while her car was out of commission.

And then there was that kiss. That sweet, innocent, unexpected kiss that had her body tingling long after they pulled apart. She had no idea what possessed him to cover her mouth with his, but since he hadn't made a big deal about the gesture, Rayne tried not to either. That didn't mean that she hadn't thought about it every day since.

There was just something about Jerry. He was hard to resist. Sure, he was good-looking, nice and had a wonderful sense of humor, but it was more than that. He was overwhelmingly intriguing. He had a way with people, making everyone he met feel as if they were the most important person in the world. At least that's how he made her feel.

"Mommy, can I go and get Jerry?"

"No, Stormy. I told him what time we're eating. He'll be here shortly," Rayne said, flipping the pancakes and then scrambling the eggs. The bacon was ready and she had placed the fruit salad on the table. A few more minutes and everything would be done.

"But Mommy, Jerry likes it when I go to his house and help him come over. Can I go?"

Rayne shook her head and laughed at her daughter's serious expression just as they heard Jerry's signature knock on the front door. Stormy ran off in a sprint.

"Don't open that door until you look out the window and make sure it's him."

Seconds later, Rayne didn't have to look over her shoulder to know that Jerry had entered her home. Like usual, her body tingled from the top of her head to the soles of her feet, and the heat that soared through her veins was enough to set fire to a flame-retardant blanket.

What the heck was it about this man, that whenever he was within ten feet, her body immediately responded? This was why she had to keep her wits when around him. He might make her feel like a gorgeous goddess with just a look, but Rayne hated the silent power he had over her. It pissed her off. He probably made every woman he encountered feel the same way. None of them stood a chance against the hot blooded, sexy as sin, man.

Just like they hadn't been able to resist Kirk.

Frustration pulsed through Rayne's body at the thought of her late husband.

I will not succumb to another player.

The words played over and over in her head as she finished scrambling the eggs.

I will not succumb to another player.

Rayne put the eggs in a bowl and set the dish on the counter, but then her gaze slammed into Jerry. And as usual, his intense eyes trailed the length of her body as if seeing her for the first time. She suddenly wished that she had taken more care in dressing. Opting for comfort, Rayne had chosen an oversize, black long-sleeved T-shirt and yoga pants. He looked at her as if he was peeling off her clothes in slow motion with only his eyes.

So much for the chant. The sexual tension between them was getting stronger by the day and despite Rayne's efforts to keep him at a distance, she wanted him. God help her. She wanted him in every way a woman wanted a man.

"What's wrong, Mommy?" Stormy asked, perched in Jerry's arms. Rayne's heart did a giddy-up at the sweet picture they made just standing there.

"I was um…checking to see if Jerry looked any older since it's his birthday."

Stormy studied him critically. "He looks the same to me."

Rayne and Jerry laughed, and the tension was effectively broken, until Stormy asked him, "How old are you?"

Jerry tweaked her nose. "I'm twenty-eight."

Rayne groaned internally. *He's so young.* Yet another reason why she didn't need to be thinking about him as more than a friend. She could add the five-year age difference to the list of all the reasons why she would never succumb to Jerry Jenkins.

"Oh, happy birthday," Rayne finally said.

He smiled and her heart rate doubled. *Geesh.*

"Thanks, babe. It smells good in here."

Stormy laughed. "You called her, babe."

Jerry grimaced and looked at Rayne. "Sorry about that," he mumbled. That twinkle in his eyes didn't look like he was sorry, but he probably hadn't meant to use the term of endearment in front of her child.

Rayne pulled the orange juice from the refrigerator. "Hungry?" she asked Jerry who was leaning against the kitchen counter. Arms folded across his chest, brought attention to his thick biceps, and the gray T-shirt straining against them.

"I'm always hungry."

"Great, then we can all sit down and eat."

For the next half an hour, they ate, talked and laughed as if the three of them had breakfast together all the time. The moment felt surreal. Like they were a family. This was what Rayne had dreamed of having with Kirk, but their marriage had hit rock bottom before it got going good. She might not have any intention of ever getting married again, but she'd be lying if she said that she wasn't enjoying this moment.

"Ow," Stormy whined, catching Rayne's attention.

"What's wrong?"

"My teeth hurt." Stormy wiggled the loose front tooth that had been bothering her off and on for the last couple of days. Considering how much it was wiggling under her touch, it would probably fall out before the day was over.

"Want me to pull it for you?" Jerry asked, reaching for Stormy. She leaned away from him, practically falling out of the chair with a look of horror on her face.

"Nooo," she cried, tears filling her eyes.

"Maybe you should let him pull it out, Stormy. Then it'll stop hurting."

"And you'll get a visit from the tooth fairy," Jerry added.

Rayne groaned. She'd had no intention of mentioning the tooth fairy idea, but by the way her daughter perked up, it was too late.

"Anna got five dollars from the tooth fairy when her tooth came out," Stormy said, the tears miraculously disappearing as she talked about the neighbor, Mrs. Addy's, granddaughter.

Jerry went back to eating. "You'll probably get more money than Anna received since Anna—"

"Jerry," Rayne snapped, not wanting to encourage the route this conversation was going. One, she wasn't supporting the tooth fairy idea. Two, she didn't want him

57

saying anything bad about Anna, especially not in front of Stormy who would most definitely repeat it.

"What?" he asked innocently. "It's true. Anna is a little terror, and Ladybug is a sweetheart. I'm sure the tooth fairy will take that into consideration when she doles out cash."

"What does dole mean?" Stormy asked.

Jerry had her complete attention while he explained how the tooth fairy operated. He really was good with Stormy, but clearly Rayne needed to talk to him. She hadn't grown up believing in the tooth fairy, Santa Claus or any other fictitious characters and hadn't planned on introducing them to Stormy.

Then again, Rayne's childhood had been downright miserable. A time in her life that she would never want to revisit. Maybe she shouldn't rule out Jerry's method just yet. She had always said that she wanted Stormy's childhood to be special. Special enough for her to look back on it with fond memories.

Once they were done with breakfast and had decided to let Stormy's tooth fall out naturally, Jerry opened the birthday gifts that they'd picked up for him. The *You're the Best!* key chain that Stormy had given him and the *Electricians do their best work in the dark* travel mug from Rayne, had been a hit.

A short while later, Stormy went to her room to make her bed.

"Did you get enough to eat?" Rayne asked Jerry as they cleared the table and carried the dirty dishes the short distance to the kitchen.

"Yeah, I'm good." He patted his flat abs, drawing Rayne's attention to them.

Considering he was a big eater, it was amazing that he was so fit. From what she'd seen of his sexy body, he didn't have any fat anywhere.

"Breakfast was delicious. Feel free to cook for me anytime."

She gave an unladylike snort. "Yeah, I'll keep that in mind." She loved cooking and often set a plate aside for him, especially when he worked late.

Jerry handed her the dirty dishes and Rayne lowered them into the hot dishwater. Her body stiffened when he stood behind her, and he leaned in close.

"It's true you know," he crooned, his voice deeper than it had been moments ago.

"Wh—what?" she croaked, barely recognizing her own voice as he caged her in, his hands gripping the counter on either side of her. His enticing, woodsy scent enfolded Rayne like a cashmere blanket, making her weak in the knees.

God, he smelled good. But she refused to let him see how much he affected her and kept her back to him. "What's true?" Her voice sounded stronger than she felt while being engulfed in the intensity of his presence.

"That electricians do their best work in the dark. I can prove it to you if you'd like," he purred close to her ear causing her to shiver.

Trying not to touch him, Rayne turned to face him, but bumped into his chest. His powerful, wide chest. "Um, you're crowding me." She pushed against said chest and immediately regretted the move. Heat blossomed through her body. She had no desire to remove her hands.

Just push him away...or go beneath his arms...or...do something, she chastised herself to no avail. This was what she meant by the power that he had over her. For a person who had common sense, at least most of the time, Rayne was currently proving otherwise. He felt so good, that the desire to touch more of him overshadowed her good judgment.

"I've dreamed about having your hands on my body," he admitted, and made his pecs bounce up and down under her touch.

Rayne gasped and dropped her hands as if handling something hot. Jerry chuckled but didn't step away. If anything, he moved closer. Too close. Close enough for her to raise up on her tip-toes and kiss his full, and oh so sexy lips if she wanted to.

But I don't want to…right?

Who was she kidding? She definitely wanted to kiss him. The last time had been mind-boggling and too quick, making her curious. Deep down, she definitely wanted to taste his lips again.

I'm sure it would be good…but I can't. I won't. She argued with herself.

I will not succumb to another player.

*

"What if I asked you to go out to dinner with me, like on a date tonight. What would you say?" Jerry asked when Rayne turned and went back to washing dishes.

"I'd ask why."

"You know why."

Her hands stalled in the sudsy water and she glanced at him. "No, actually, I don't know why. Jerry, you and I are neighbors…and friends. That's it. Like I've already told you, I'm not looking for anything more than that in my life right now."

"What you mean is that you're not looking for anything more than that with me."

She rinsed a plate and set it in the dish rack. "I said exactly what I meant. Raising Stormy in a healthy and loving environment is my number one goal. I don't have time for anything else."

"You don't have time because you're not trying to make time. What about your needs Rayne? I'm sure you can use a night out on occasion or some adult entertainment from time to time. Why not go—"

"My needs don't matter. All that matters is Stormy. I owe her the chance to have the best possible childhood, and I plan on giving her that."

Jerry stared, willing her to look at him, but she didn't. Rayne turned back to the sink. When she finished washing the last plate and dried her hands, he stopped her from moving to the stove by tugging on the front of the oversize shirt and pulling her to him.

"You are an amazing mother. There's no denying that. Actually, it's one of many things I like about you," he said when she finally met his gaze. Each time she looked at him with those beautiful light brown eyes, he lost a little more of his heart to her. "I would never do anything that would hinder you from taking care of Stormy. But who takes care of you? It's all well and good that you feel that your sole purpose in life is your child, but what about you, Rayne?"

"What about me? I don't matter right now. All that matters—"

"You matter to me, and it pisses me the hell off that you would even say something like that."

"Jerry."

"Rayne."

She released a dramatic sigh and her shoulders drooped like a deflated balloon, but she didn't pull away from him.

"The last few months of hanging out with you and Stormy have been fun. And for the first time in my life, I look forward to arriving home, knowing there's a good chance that I'll see you two. But somewhere along the way, my feelings for you guys have grown and—"

"Jerry, I'm not denying that we don't love hanging out with you, too. I'll admit, you and Stormy are the highlights of my day. Her exuberant energy and love for life, and your humor and kindness make me forget the trials that go with being a working, single mother. But I think we should keep things the way they are between you and me. Dating will only complicate things between us."

"I don't think it will. You already know how much you and Stormy mean to me, but I want you to be more than my neighbor and my friend. I want us to get to know each other better. I want—"

"We don't always get what we want," she snapped, then placed her hand on her chest and huffed out a breath. "I'm proof of that. Since I was a little girl, I wanted to be a part of a loving family. When that didn't happen, I had every intention of having my own family. I married the first man who made me feel special, and then I got pregnant. I wanted a fairytale life of happily-ever-after. Instead, my husband turned out to be a selfish bastard who didn't give a crap about me and then got himself killed. Now I'm raising the most precious little girl by myself and struggling to keep up with…" She stopped abruptly and stiffened. She glanced away feverishly wiping away tears that suddenly slipped from her eyes.

Selfish bastard? Killed? Struggling?

What the hell?

His chest tightened when a tear slipped down her face and then another. "Finish what you were going to say," he prodded gently, caressing her damp cheek with the pad of his thumb.

He had sensed something was up the week before, and this declaration was more proof. Maybe she was just overwhelmed with all of her responsibilities and needed a break. All the more reason to take her out on the town for a night of fun.

"Tell me what's going on. Maybe I can help."

She tried pulling away, but Jerry maintained his hold on the front of her shirt. "I'm sorry…there's nothing to tell. I said more than I intended to."

Instead of pushing for a better explanation, Jerry wrapped his arms around her and she laid her head against his chest. Placing a kiss on top of her head, he recalled something his mother once said.

Sometimes all you need is a hug to make the cloudiest day brighter.

Chapter Eight

Engulfed in Jerry's tender embrace, Rayne steadied her breathing. Why had she snapped at him? He'd asked her out plenty of times and usually they kept the conversation light, but today...

She hadn't intended to tell him anything about Kirk or her financial situation. Yet, that's exactly what happened. No doubt he'd have questions, but she was grateful he wasn't pushing for answers. So much for keeping her emotions in check and her personal life private. Now he knew that her world wasn't as peachy as she wanted him to believe.

"You're no good to anyone, especially Stormy, if you're not taking care of yourself or if you're unhappy," he said softly against her hair. "Let me take you out for dinner. No pressure. No date. We'll have a great meal, do some dancing, and I'll even tell a few jokes."

Rayne laughed. "I've heard some of your jokes," she mumbled against his chest before lifting her head. "They're not that good."

Laughing, Jerry kissed her cheek and flashed that grin that always sent butterflies fluttering inside of her belly.

"Well, I guess I need to work on some new material." He cupped her cheek and she couldn't help but lean into his touch. "You okay?" he asked.

"Yeah, I'm fine. Sorry about that."

"You don't have to apologize to me. Just know that if you ever want to talk. I'm here for you."

Warmth traveled through her body at the affection in his eyes. Then his gaze dropped lower, to her mouth. It was as if Rayne could read his mind, knowing that he wanted to kiss her. Or maybe it was her mind, nudging her to lean in more and taste his tempting lips.

"There's something I've wanted to do from the moment I walked in here this morning."

Without another word, he covered her mouth with his, and Rayne's brain short-circuited. Her mind screamed stop, don't do this, move away, but she couldn't. She craved to be kissed, touched, and held. And with the way Jerry held her and devoured her mouth, he knew how to do all of the above.

And damn if his mouth didn't feel good against hers.

The kiss stole her breath away, and Rayne held on tight to the front of his T-shirt, trying to ignore the warning bells sounding in her head. She loved the way he took charge, taking what he wanted and giving her what she needed.

Still, the thought of kissing her neighbor...her friend...her...Jerry, sent a wave of elation mixed with fear warring within her.

Don't think. Just be.

The words rattled in her mind, but battled with her common sense while her body was on high alert. Rayne wasn't a small woman, but wrapped in Jerry's strong, muscular arms, she felt dainty and desired. It had been a long time since a man made her feel so good.

"Jerry!"

Stormy's high pitched scream pierced the quietness of the house, and Rayne's heart leaped into her throat. She and Jerry jerked apart, and before she could get her feet to move, he took off in a sprint toward the stairs. By the time either of them touched the first step, Stormy was half way down the staircase.

"My tooth came out!" she screeched, waving her fisted hand in the air, her little legs carrying her quickly toward them.

Jerry blew out a breath and placed his hand over his chest. "She scared the heck out of me," he said only loud enough for Rayne to hear.

"Yeah, welcome to my world." Her chest heaved while she willed her heart rate to go back to normal. "She's easily excited."

"Look," Stormy said animatedly, her high-pitched voice loud enough to break glass, and then she leaped into Jerry's arms. "It came out all by itself. See."

He kissed her cheek and opened his hand for her to drop the tiny tooth into his palm. "Yeah, I see. Let's give it to mommy so you don't lose it before the tooth fairy visits."

"Jerry," Rayne warned, not wanting him to encourage the tooth fairy fantasy, but he ignored her. His sole focus was on her child.

"Grab something for us to put this in," he said, handing Rayne the tooth and then gently tugged on Stormy's chin. "Open up, Ladybug. Let me see."

There wasn't much blood, but Rayne stood back and observed as he rinsed her daughter's mouth with warm water. Normally a girlie-girl and squeamish when it came to blood and pain, Stormy was taking everything in stride, listening as Jerry talked to her in a calm voice. Telling her that eventually more of her baby teeth would fall out but that they would all grow back fast. Through it all, he held her in his arms, carrying her around, something that Stormy always enjoyed.

Like Rayne, most of her friends didn't have fathers in their lives. Which was why she appreciated the time Jerry spent with Stormy. He might have his faults, like everyone did, but he went beyond the call of duty for her daughter. And Rayne had no doubt he would one day be an amazing father.

He put Stormy on her feet. "All right. You're all set."

"Now the tooth fairy will come?"

"Yup, but not until you go to sleep tonight. Tomorrow morning you'll be a little richer."

"Does that mean I'm going to get five dollars like Anna got?"

Rayne narrowed her eyes at Jerry, trying to subliminally tell him not to promise something she might not be able to deliver.

"You'll have to wait and see," he said. "We never know how much the tooth fairy will leave."

The song, *Here Comes the Sun,* rang out through the kitchen and Jerry dug his ringing cell phone out of his pocket.

"Who is it?" Stormy asked, tugging on his arm.

"It's my mother. She's probably calling to wish me a happy birthday."

"Can I talk to your mommy?" Stormy asked excitedly. "What's her name?"

Jerry laughed. "Her name is Violet."

"That's Mrs. Jenkins to you," Rayne added and scowled at him, only making him laugh again.

"I'm sure my mom would love to talk to you. Here." To Rayne's surprise, he handed the phone to Stormy.

"Hello?" Stormy said, and strolled into the living room with the device.

"You do know that she's going to talk your mother's ear off, right? What if the call is important?"

"Actually, my mother will probably do most of the talking. She'll get a kick out of Ladybug." He stood in front of Rayne. "So, let's talk about that kiss."

*

Before Rayne could respond, Stormy skipped back into the kitchen holding up his cell phone.

"Jerry, your mommy is almost here," she said, bouncing up and down, grinning. "She's going to meet me."

He frowned and reached for the phone. "Hey, mom. What's up?"

"Happy birthday, baby," she chirped in her usual sing-song voice.

A smile tilted the corners of Jerry's mouth. She was the only person he knew who was happy every single day, and it showed in her voice and the way she treated people.

"Thank you. How are you this morning?" he asked, glancing down at Stormy who looked at him expectantly.

"I'm wonderful. I was trying to be the first person to call and tell you happy birthday, but I guess Stormy beat me too it. She sounds like a doll. Now I know why you're so taken with her. I'm looking forward to finally meeting her and Rayne."

Jerry's gaze followed Rayne around the first floor as she tidied up. He talked about her and Stormy often in conversation, but had only told Liam about wanting to date her. "Hopefully, I can make that happen one day," he said to his mother.

"How about now? Your sister and I are outside."

"What?"

Apparently Stormy had been right. With his phone plastered against his ear, Jerry headed to the door. "Mom, I thought we talked about you not dropping by unannounced. Why didn't you call me earlier?"

"I know, I know, sweetie. I shouldn't be just dropping by out of the blue, but this is a special occasion. It's your birthday."

"It's not that big of a deal." The moment the words left his mouth, he wanted to pull them back. When they were kids, she prided herself on making his and his sisters' birthdays special. Each celebration topped the previous year, making them the envy of all of their friends.

She tsked. "Every day we're alive is a big deal. None of us are promised tomorrow. That's why we have to appreciate and celebrate each year God gives us."

"Yeah, you're right." He opened the door. On the concrete stoop that was between his and Rayne's place, stood his mother and his sister, Christina.

Stormy slid past him before he could stop her. "Hi. Are you Jerry's mommy?"

Violet stooped down and hugged her. "Oh my, God. You are absolutely adorable. Yes, I'm Jerry's mommy and you must be Stormy."

Jerry smiled, watching as they discussed each other's outfit. His mother's style was a throwback to her hippie days. Today her long, curly hair was held back with a floral headband, and her outfit consisted of an oversize buttoned up checkered shirt and a long floral skirt and flip flops.

Now that he thought about it, Stormy had a similar style whenever Rayne let her dress herself, like today. She had paired a wrinkled, flowy, prairie style blouse with denim short shorts and pink cowboy boots.

Jerry glanced at Christina who was also dressed like their mother. She was two years older than him and stood there grinning like she knew a secret.

"Happy birthday, my brotha." She hugged him, handing him a blue envelope before whispering in his ear. "You know mom's gonna want to adopt her, right? Or worse, insist on one of us giving her some more grandkids."

"Yeah, you and Luke need to get on that," he said of her husband.

Violet absolutely adored kids and would've had more herself if she could've. With only two grandchildren so far, thanks to their sister, Peyton, their mother impatiently waited for more.

"Jerry said you were a cutie-pie, and he was right," Violet said.

"He calls me his Ladybug. What's your name?" Stormy asked Christina.

"Everyone calls me CJ."

"Oh. My mommy's name is Rayne. Wanna meet her?" Stormy ran off before they could answer, and they all burst out laughing.

"She has a lot of energy," Christina said and Jerry agreed.

He wasn't sure how Rayne would react to meeting part of his family, but he would love to introduce them. Within seconds, Stormy dragged Rayne to the door and his pulse amped up at the sight of her. It didn't matter that he had just spent the last hour with her.

What a sap. But I don't even care.

He draped his arm around Rayne's shoulder. "This is my mother Violet Jenkins and my sister, Christina Jenkins-Hayden. You guys this is Rayne Ellison."

"It's nice to finally meet you. I hope you don't mind, but I'm a hugger," Violet said.

"I don't mind at all."

They hugged and Jerry's heart rate sped up a little. Seeing his favorite women together felt surreal, like it was the beginning of a future he'd been dreaming about. One big happy family.

"It's nice meeting you both. Would you like to come in?" Rayne asked, shocking Jerry a little. She was kind-hearted, but he hadn't been sure how she'd react to the intrusion.

"That would be great, if you don't mind," Violet said. "Jerry's always getting on me about stopping by unannounced."

"It's no problem. Come on in." Rayne escorted them inside and Jerry followed.

For the next thirty minutes, they sat in the family room talking and laughing at Stormy's antics. She was in her element, prancing around and rattling off one question after another to his mother and sister.

"Forgive my manners. Would either of you like something to drink? Coffee? Juice?" Rayne asked.

"Coffee sounds good," Christina said.

Rayne turned to Violet who was holding Stormy in her lap.

"Just water for me. Thanks," she said.

Jerry followed Rayne into the kitchen. "Sorry about the imposition, but thank you for welcoming them." He spoke only loud enough for her to hear.

"No problem. They seem really nice."

"I'm glad you think so." He poured his mother a glass of water from the Brita pitcher that was in the refrigerator. "If you and I move forward with dinner tonight, I know my parents wouldn't mind watching Ladybug. And I promise they're the best."

"Jerry." She drew out his name, frowning as if struggling with herself. That's when he knew she was softening to the idea of going out.

"I promise we'll have a good time tonight."

After a long hesitation, she said, "*Fine*. You win. I'm only going out to dinner with you because it's your birthday, and we better have a good time."

Jerry smiled, not missing the humor in her voice.

"We will. I promise."

Chapter Nine

"What do you mean he kissed you? Are we talking a sweet little peck on the lips? Or are we talking holding you close and palming your ass while making mad, passionate love to your mouth, and leaving you panting for more?"

Rayne's mouth dropped open. "Really, Charlee? You do realize kids are running around here, right?"

Charlee pushed back the colorful headband that was holding her wild, auburn curls out of her face. "Just answer the question."

Rayne thoughts drifted to Jerry, their conversation in the kitchen, and the fact that she had agreed to go to dinner with him. Instead of responding to her friend, her gaze swept over the McDonald's where they were having lunch and catching up with each other's lives. Stormy was nearby, running around the play area, having a blast with other children.

"Your silence speaks volumes," Charlee said. "I'm still trying to wrap my brain around all of this. I can't believe you kissed Jerry "Jay" Jenkins. The gorgeous man who looks as if his body was carved by a master sculptor and then hand dipped in rich, dark chocolate."

Rayne smiled at her friend's description and its accuracy. She also had to admit that Jerry had mad kissing skills. He had taken his time, savored her mouth and had definitely left her wanting more.

Rayne picked at her salad. No matter how many excuses she came up with for why it wasn't a good idea to get involved with him, she couldn't deny their attraction.

"Explain to me again how this kiss came about."

"You heard me. It just...happened."

"I hate when people say that crap. A hot, juicy ass kiss doesn't just happen," she retorted, her mouth twitching to hold back a smile. "Unless he held you *and* your face down, you had a chance to move your lips before his mouth landed on them. I'm just...floored. Ms. Buttoned-Up-Tight finally let a man kiss her, and I'm sure you kissed him back."

"I didn't. Well, not exactly," she defended weakly. She hadn't been kissed in like...forever, especially not like Jerry had taken control of her mouth. She also hadn't had sex in years. Of course, she would have a weakness for the first man to show an interest in her. Well, a weakness for one of the men who showed interest. There was also Calvin. But with him, there was a different type of attraction. Not a sexual one.

"Jerry might have initiated the kiss, but you didn't push him away. You wanted that kiss. You *want* him. And I'm pretty sure that blush tinting your cheeks is not makeup. Come on, admit it," Charlee taunted, shoveling fries into her mouth.

The woman could put away more food than most men. Yet, she didn't gain a pound. Rayne usually stayed away from fried food and opted for at least one or two salads a day, but couldn't lose the extra pounds she was carrying around.

"I'm not admitting anything," she said, picking at her salad with fruit and chicken on top of it. What she really wanted was a double cheese burger, fries and an apple pie. But she was determined to lose some weight.

"I knew it. You liked it."

Rayne more than liked the kiss. She was going to be dreaming about how good Jerry's lips felt against hers until the end of time. The moment his mouth landed on hers and he pulled her close to his hard body, she'd been a goner.

"I just can't let it happen again."

Charlee blew out a sigh and pointed her last fry at Rayne. "Sometimes I don't understand you. Here you have this gorgeous, hot man who will worship the ground you walk on if you'd let him, but you keep shooting him down. Who does that?"

"What do you mean who does that? You're the one who told me about his reputation. You're the one who told me that he's rarely seen with the same woman twice. You're also the one who told me that women fawn over him. Why would I subject myself to that, especially after what Kirk put me through?"

"To be fair, I told you what I've heard about Jerry in the past. But from what you've told me about Kirk, he and Jerry are very different."

"And you know this how?" Rayne said with more edge in her tone than intended. She braced herself. Was her best friend going to tell her that she'd been with Jerry?

"Okay, I'll admit, I don't really know Jerry. But I've heard some really nice things about him, and I know his family. Well, I don't really *know* them, but I know of them."

"Really? How is it that I didn't know that?"

"I-I…it…it doesn't matter. All that matters is… You know what? Maybe you should tell me everything that happened this morning. I'm gonna need all the details, and don't leave anything out."

Rayne told her friend about Jerry's birthday breakfast, Stormy's tooth, and how they met Jerry's mother and his youngest sister. Rayne didn't know what she expected before meeting the women, but they both were like a breath of fresh air, acting as if they'd known her and Stormy forever. She hadn't met Jerry's father or his oldest sister, Peyton, but she already knew that he was blessed to have such wonderful people in his life.

"Soo, you told Jerry about Kirk."

"Not exactly. I might or might not have called Kirk a selfish bastard, and I might've said something about not letting another man make a fool of me."

"Ah, I see. So you were being nice and didn't tell him what Kirk was really like, huh?"

Rayne covered her face with her hands and groaned before dropping them back to the table. "Trust me. I said way more than I should've. I even eluded to the fact that I was barely keeping a roof over our heads."

Thankfully, Jerry hadn't asked her to expound on that topic. The last thing she wanted was his pity. Or knowing him, he would've offered to loan her money or worse, pay her bills or buy her a house. No, he'd done enough for them over the months. She was the one responsible for seeing to her and her daughter's needs.

"For what it's worth, I don't think Jerry is anything like Kirk. Well, not exactly. They might have similar reputations, but I never heard of Jerry mistreating anyone or leading anyone on. Not that I know everything about him mind you, but I know his family. Uh, sort of."

"Okay, spill. That's the second time you've eluded to knowing his family. What do you know? Or who do you know?"

"Girl, don't mind me. Jenkins & Sons has done work for my father a number of times, and he speaks very highly of the family. Personally, I've only met a couple of them, and they seem like good people."

Charlee was hiding something. God only knew what. Growing up, her friend used to be what people back in the day called a wild child. She'd try anything once and got into more trouble than anyone Rayne knew, and didn't mellow out until her mother died while they were in high school. After that, Rayne didn't see much of her since Charlee's father moved her to Cincinnati.

"Okay, so what are you wearing tonight?" Charlee asked. "Because what you have on now won't work."

Rayne glanced down at the baggy, purple shirt and stretch pants. "Yeah, I'm going to have to dig through my closet and see what I can pull together."

Rayne hadn't been on a date since before marrying Kirk, and even then, it hadn't been many. The dressiest outfit she owned was a maxi dress that she purchased during her pregnancy and a really nice interview suit she had found at Goodwill years ago.

"I'm sure you have nothing appropriate for a date. Let's go shopping after we leave here."

When Charlee wasn't working, she was shopping. The fashionista, rarely did she leave home without looking cute. Like now. The red halter sundress and strappy sandals looked amazing on her.

"Girl, I don't have money for shopping. I'll pull something together."

"I have a better idea. We go shopping and I can buy you an early birthday gift."

"Early? Charlee, my birthday is not for another five months. That's beyond early."

Charlee waved her off. "Whatever. We're going. Or you could always get Stormy to find you something to wear. That little girl already has her own style. Look at her. Anyone who can put short shorts and cowboy boots together, and look cute in it, is a fashionista in my book."

Rayne laughed. "More like a hippie in the making. Did you see that little pink flower in her hair? I don't know where she found it, but after she begged me to let her wear her hair down, the flower miraculously appeared. She told me she wanted to look pretty for Jerry's birthday."

Charlee shook her head and grinned. "You have a special little girl there. She's smart, adorable, and resourceful."

"You're her godmother. Your opinion is a little biased."

"Maybe, but it's all true. Look at her over there. I wonder what happened to her friend."

Stormy was standing near the door that led into the play area. She made a buddy wherever she went, and the little girl she'd been playing with was now crying, pointing to the slide that was inside of the enclosure.

"Her friend's father is kind of cute."

"And probably married," Rayne said absently, wondering what had happened. Since Stormy seemed fine, she stayed seated to see how the scene would play out. The father was talking to his daughter while wiping her tears. Before long, the little girl seemed fine while he helped her into her shoes shortly before they left.

Stormy headed to the table. Normally, she ran like a ball of energy everywhere she went, but not this time. Right now, she looked deep in thought, or as deep in thought as a five-year-old could look.

"What's wrong, sweetheart?" Rayne hugged her daughter's petite body. "What happened to your friend?"

"She hurt her leg and started crying. She wanted her daddy, and when he hugged her, she stopped crying."

Rayne and Stormy watched as the little girl and her father walked out of the building hand in hand.

Rayne squeezed Stormy's shoulder. "Are you done playing?"

"Yes," she murmured, and turned troubled eyes up to Rayne. "Mommy...I want a daddy."

Charlee choked on her soda and started coughing. She patted her chest but the cough grew louder. Her shocked, watery eyes met Rayne's.

Not a day went by that Stormy didn't catch Rayne off guard with her questions, comments, and in this case, requests. But right now, she was at a loss at how to respond. On occasion, she asked questions about Kirk, but this was the first time she'd asked for a daddy.

"Can you get me one?" she asked seriously, her eyes steady on Rayne, her lips pinched together, looking much older than her five years.

"I'll be back," Charlee rasped, coughing and clearly trying to hide her laughter at the same time.

"Mommy, can you?" Stormy persisted.

"Sweetheart, why do you want a daddy?"

"Because when you're sad they pick you up and help you stop crying and...they're nice."

"Um..." Was all that came out when Rayne opened her mouth, struggling to find the right words. "Mommy's are nice to, and they wipe their children's tears. Why do—"

"I know, but I want a daddy. Can you get me one?"

"Well, it's not that simple," Rayne started, knowing that whatever she came up with wouldn't appease her child. "I have to be married before you can get a daddy."

"Can you get married?"

Her serious expression bought a smile to Rayne's face. "I was already married, and you had a daddy, but he's in he..." Rayne stopped herself. She had no idea where Kirk's soul might've ended up."

"Can you get married again and then get me another daddy?" Stormy continued.

Rayne sighed. "Honey, I...we... We'll talk about it later, okay?"

This was one of those conversations Rayne needed to think on. And no doubt the topic would come up again.

*

"I don't know about this outfit, Charlee. This looks more like something you would wear, not me." Rayne stared at herself in the full-length mirror, admiring how feminine the mustard colored, lace trim, keyhole blouse looked on her. Even though it brought attention to her full breasts, it cinched in the middle, giving the illusion of a narrow waistline. The outfit was sexy, yet tasteful. Alluring, but not too revealing.

She ran her hands down her wide hips and over the navy-blue pencil skirt, that stopped just above her knees. Would Jerry like the outfit? Was that what she wanted, for him to like the way she looked? The evening was only supposed to be about them going to dinner to celebrate his birthday. Nothing else.

Charlee stood behind her, fluffing the loose curls she had put in Rayne's hair. "If you really want Jerry to swallow his tongue, I say we pin your hair so that it falls over one shoulder like this."

Rayne let Charlee do her thing, but couldn't help wondering if it was a good idea to look so suggestive. Nothing beyond dinner was happening tonight, and she didn't want to come across as a tease. But then again, she had to admit that she like the way her neck looked with her hair swept to one side over her shoulder.

Rayne turned to face her friend and Charlee stood back grinning.

"I think you're ready. I just wish I could see the expression on the man's face when he lays eyes on you. He is going to lose his shit." She squealed.

"Language, girl. You know that little person in the other room is like a sponge, soaking up everything we say."

"Right, right. You're right." Charlee glanced at the thin watch on her wrist. "I'm going to head out. My dad wants me to stop by the office tonight since I'll be flying out early in the morning."

Her father owned the company where Rayne worked. A company that manufactured construction supplies and equipment. Charlee, a sales rep for the organization, traveled around the country.

"Stormy, where are you?" Charlee called out when they stepped out of the bedroom.

"In my room."

Rayne followed Charlee down the hall toward the bedroom and they both pulled up short at the door.

"Little girl, if you don't clean this room up right now, you won't be going anywhere. I knew you were too quiet in here. I want all of these toys in that toy box, now. It's almost time for us to leave," Rayne said. How one kid could make such a mess was a mystery to her.

Charlee kneeled down next to Stormy who was surrounded by every doll and stuffed animal she owned.

"Okay, kiddo, I'm getting ready to go. Give me a hug. I'll be out of town for a while, but you be good while I'm gone, okay?"

"Okay, Auntie Charlee." Stormy hugged her, almost knocking Charlee over. "Don't forget to buy me something," she said in a loud whisper, and Rayne shook her head.

"Don't I always?" Charlee whispered back just as loudly.

"Stormy, when you finish this room, put your pajamas and your toothbrush in your backpack to take over to Mr. and Mrs. Jenkins' house."

"Am I spending the night?"

"No, but it might be late when we pick you up, and I want you to be ready for bed. I'm going to walk Auntie Charlee to the door. Make sure this room is clean by the time I come back upstairs."

"Okay." Stormy started picking up toys. "Mommy?" she called before Rayne and Charlee stepped into the hallway.

"Yes."

"Is it too late to get Jerry a puppy for his birthday?"

Oh good, Lord. Not the puppy thing again.

"Yes, it's too late, and he loves the gifts we picked out," Rayne said, her mind immediately going back to what he said about proving that electricians did their best work in the dark. When she purchased the mug, she knew he would get a kick out of the innuendo, but hadn't planned to fuel Jerry's flirtatious nature. Yet, that's exactly what it had done.

"But I think Jerry really wants a puppy," Stormy pressed. "He talks about puppies all the time."

"Only because you keep bringing it up. He's not the one who wants a dog, you are. And we've already talked about why you're not getting one yet. Now clean your room." Rayne walked out before more questions came.

"That girl is a trip," Charlee said, laughing as they went down the stairs.

"That's putting it mildly. She's getting to be a real handful."

"And you love her to death."

Rayne smiled and headed to the front door. "You know it. She's my everything."

"All right, I'm out of here. Have fun tonight and do everything that I would do."

Rayne laughed. "Um, I don't think so. Doing something your wild tail would do could land me in trouble. I'm only going out to dinner and that's it."

"Fine, but for the love of God, please order something other than a salad. You drive me nuts with that crap. Would it kill you to order a juicy steak and potatoes or some ribs for a change?"

"Whatever. Just go." They hugged at the door before opening it. Rayne always missed her friend when she traveled, and would probably miss her even more since she was going to be gone for several weeks. "Call while you're away and be safe."

"Always."

Chapter Ten

Jerry leaned on the breakfast bar and stared down at the blueprint, in awe of what his cousin Liam had come up with.

"This is exactly what I envisioned. Ladybug is going to freak when this is all done."

Liam finished the bottle of water and tossed it in the recycle bin. "I'm glad you approve. I have to admit. I never thought you would ever ask me to draw up plans for a doll house. Why not just buy one?"

Liam, an architect, normally spent his time designing impressive plans for homes or multi-million-dollar office buildings. This was the first time anyone had ever commissioned him to draw up plans for a doll house.

"I considered buying one, but I wanted her to have a one of a kind. Now, I just hope we thought of everything. It has to be perfect." He couldn't explain it, but he wanted Stormy to have something from him that she'd remember even after she was grown and on her own.

"Trust me, you've thought of everything, including track lighting in the family room. And I can't say that I've ever seen a dollhouse that's a side-by-side townhouse."

"I know right? I thought she'd love a smaller version of our townhomes."

He and Rayne might live next door to each other, but their places had different floor plans. Jerry had three levels with three bedrooms and three and a half bathrooms. Rayne's had two levels with only two bedrooms and one and a half bathrooms. Based on the drawing, Liam had captured even the smallest details.

"It was a good idea to include the handle and the two doors as well as the lock just in case the house has to be moved. Now, I just hope MJ can get it built before Christmas," Jerry said, still looking over the blueprint.

Their cousin, Martina, was one of the best carpenters in the city and often did intricate woodworking projects on the side. She assured him that even though she hadn't built one, she could handle the miniature-size project.

"Christmas is not for another six months. I've seen her knock out some pretty big jobs in less time. I'm sure she can get this done. Even if she doesn't, come Christmas, you can always take Stormy over there to see whatever is done."

"True, but it wouldn't be the same. Nah, I need it done before Christmas, even if it means I have to help build it."

"Don't you think this is a little much for the little girl, especially not knowing if you'll ever get with her mom?"

Jerry rolled the blueprint and held it up. "This has nothing to do with Rayne. I want Stormy to have something special from me." Deep down he wanted both Rayne and Stormy in his life forever. But if things didn't work out between him and Rayne, he'd still be in Stormy's life.

Liam nodded. "All right, well, when am I going to meet this neighbor lady and your ladybug? Considering how much you bring their names into every conversation, I feel like I already know them."

"Hopefully I can introduce you soon, but right now, I need to finish getting ready."

"Yeah, actually, I need to get out of here." Liam pulled his car keys from his pants pocket and headed to the stairs.

Jerry followed. He had twenty minutes until he picked up Rayne and Stormy, and he felt like a kid on Christmas Eve.

Anticipation drummed through his veins. He had one shot to show Rayne a good time in the hopes that she'd want them to spend more time together. Besides that, he also wanted to get her talking. As a very private person, she didn't share much. He hoped to change that tonight. He wanted her to know that she could trust and depend on him.

"Okay man, I'll catch you later," Liam said when they got to the first floor of the townhouse."

"Sounds good, and thanks again for the work you put into that drawing. You outdid yourself. Send me the invoice whenever you want, and I'll take care of it."

Liam opened the door. "Who knows, maybe this dollhouse project will turn into some..." His voice trailed off, and he froze in the doorway.

"What's up?" Jerry looked past him. Rayne's friend Charlee stood rooted in place staring at them. But it was Rayne who snagged Jerry's attention.

He elbowed Liam out of the way. "Wow, babe," Jerry said, giving her a once over. Those exquisite light-brown eyes popped more than usual with the smoky eyeshadow and bold eyeliner. She had a mysterious vibe. And rarely did she wear her hair down, but today her long, silky locks were begging for him to run his fingers through them.

His gaze went lower, taking in her bodacious figure in the body-hugging outfit, and those legs. Those long, shapely legs had his mouth watering. Hell, it was the whole package that left him almost speechless.

"You...you're absolutely stunning."

The left corner of her red lips kicked up into a smile. "Thank you."

"Liam," Charlee said, surprise in her tone. A tone that snatched Jerry's attention, bringing him back to the current situation.

"Charlee," Liam responded dryly. He sounded disinterested, but the way his appreciative gaze took her in said otherwise.

Interesting.

Jerry had met Charlee on numerous occasions, but she never mentioned knowing Liam. And considering how familiar they seemed with each other and the tension transpiring between them, he sensed a history there.

"You two know each other?" he asked, looking from one to the other.

"Yeah, unfortunately," Liam hissed.

Unease swept through Jerry. His cousin was a quiet, introvert by nature. Never rude, especially to a woman. *Especially a beautiful woman.*

Seconds ticked by as they stood there. He and Rayne observed the two enemies, waiting to see if either would expound on Liam's comment. Neither spoke. They just stood there glaring at each other. Well, Liam was glaring while Charlee watched him carefully before lowering her gaze.

Liam turned to Jerry and held up his arm, giving him a fist bump. "Check you later." He started to walk away, but Jerry caught the back of his shirt.

"Hold up, man. Let me introduce you to Rayne." He rested his hand at the small of her back. "Rayne, this is my cousin Liam. Liam, this is Rayne."

Liam extended his hand. "Nice to finally meet you."

"Thanks, you too," she said.

"You guys have a good time tonight," he said walking away.

"Dare I ask how you two know each other?" Rayne said to Charlee.

"Long story," she said, and looked at Jerry. "Show my friend a good time tonight, and don't let her order a salad. She needs a little fun in her life."

"Fun and no salad. Got it."

As she walked to her car parked in the driveway, Jerry said to Rayne, "I'll be right back."

He jogged over to Liam who had just climbed into his Chevy Camaro. He slid to a stop on the driver's side. "Hold up, man."

"Don't ask," his cousin spat before Jerry could even form a question.

With the car window down, Jerry leaned on the door. "That was pretty intense back there. You all right?"

Liam glanced to where Charlee was backing her car out of the driveway. "Yeah, I'm good. Just a little surprised to see her. I know she's an only child. So, what is she to Rayne?"

"Best friends."

Liam bobbed his head up and down but didn't comment.

"What is she to you? Someone you dated?" Jerry asked cautiously, knowing there was a good chance Liam wouldn't share any details.

Liam slipped on his aviator shades and seconds ticked by, the silence between them growing until he said, "She's my ex-fiancé,"

"Wait. What?" Jerry wasn't sure what he expected Liam to say, but it wasn't that.

"And if you want to live to see another day, you won't mention that to anyone. Now move so I can get out of here."

"Dude! You can't drop a bomb like that without details and just leave. How did I not—"

"Move your ass away from the car or get run over. Your choice," Liam barked.

Shocked by his cousin's tone, Jerry lifted his hands. He had barely got out of the way before Liam burned rubber peeling away from the curb, barely missing his feet.

"What did Charlee do?" Rayne asked when he went back to her door. "I know my friend. The expression on your face says that whatever happened wasn't good."

Jerry wanted to tell her the little that Liam shared, but whatever happened between him and Charlee was between them. At least until Liam filled him in on the details.

"He didn't say much, but you're right. Whatever happened between them wasn't good. Okay enough about them." He put his arm around her shoulders, trying to shake off the shock of what Liam had said. Questions bombarded his mind faster than he could process them, but right now, he had a non-date to finish getting dressed for.

"Ready to go?" he asked Rayne.

"I will be in ten minutes."

"Cool, I'll meet you and Ladybug out here then."

*

"All right, mom. We're going to head out. Just call if you need anything," Jerry said. With a hand at the small of her back, he guided Rayne to the front door of his parents' home. The plan had been to drop Stormy off and keep it moving, but his mother hadn't stopped talking since they walked in twenty minutes ago. He loved her, but he was ready to have Rayne to himself.

"You kids have a good time," Violet said. She and Stormy stood hand-in-hand in the doorway as Jerry and Rayne made their way down the porch stairs.

"Bye, mommy. Bye, Jerry. Have fun."

"Bye, honey. Be good for Mr. And Mrs. Jenkins." Rayne blew her a kiss.

Jerry guided her down the clay brick walkway toward his truck. "Are you sure you're all right with leaving Ladybug with my parents?" he asked, helping her into the vehicle. His gaze immediately gravitated to her gorgeous, shapely legs. He still couldn't get over her transformation. She looked very feminine and sexy as hell in the short, fitted skirt.

"Yes. I know you well enough to know that you wouldn't suggest Stormy stay with them if you didn't think she'd be well taken care of."

"I'm glad you know that," he said when he climbed into the driver's seat. "That little girl means the world to me, and I would never put her in danger."

"I know. She feels the same about you."

Rayne smiled, and an unfamiliar feeling stabbed Jerry in the chest. Knowing Rayne trusted his judgment when it came to Stormy meant everything. There was nothing he wouldn't do for her daughter. Hell, there was nothing he wouldn't do for either of them. And it didn't matter how long it took, he would prove to her the type of man he really was.

He steered his vehicle in the direction of downtown. Except for Jamison Ross's *Call Me* playing through the speakers, they rode the first ten minutes of their trip in silence. Jerry had planned a nice evening for them, starting with dinner at a seafood and steakhouse.

"Your parents are wonderful. And just the little bit of time that I've spent with your mother, I can already tell she has a beautiful spirit."

"Yeah, she's pretty cool. Although, I didn't always think so. As a kid, she used to embarrass the heck out of me without really trying. I'm sure you've noticed her unique style of dress."

Rayne grinned. "Uh, yeah. I noticed."

"She has always marched to her own beat. My friends used to always talk about how pretty she was, that she could be a model. But they'd also burst out laughing whenever they saw her in one of her outfits. Needless to say, I had my share of fights. It was okay if I had issues with her clothes, but no one else could talk about my mom."

"I assume CJ takes after her," Rayne said. "She has a similar style and a real chill vibe."

Jerry nodded, thinking about his youngest sister. "Yup, it was the same situation with her. Except my friends wanted to date her, but complained her clothes were too funny. And you're right about her personality. It usually takes a lot to get her riled."

"Does she work at Jenkins & Sons, too?"

"Yeah, she's a painter by trade and also an artist, often getting commissioned by some big-time people to do paintings for them." He didn't bother telling her that some of those paintings were super risqué.

"What about your other sister?"

"Peyton is more like my dad. She's conservative, straight-laced, and usually pretty serious. She's the most dependable and stable person you'll ever meet. She also used to drive me crazy when she ran J & S. I can't tell you how many write-ups I got from her or how many times she threatened to fire me."

Rayne laughed. "You were that bad, huh?"

"I hate to admit it, but I deserved most of those reprimands. I was young, dumb, and all about having a good time, not taking much serious, especially work."

"When you were young? You're still young," Rayne said. "Are you still cutting up at work?"

Jerry shook his head, not bothering to address the still young comment. "Nah, I finally got myself together, and stopped doing stupid stuff."

"Because you want the promotion?"

"That's partly it, but like most people, you eventually grow up and become more responsible. I know I've changed, but I'm still trying to prove myself to my cousins. A couple of them run the business, and still only see me as the punk kid who use to follow them around and cause trouble. In time they'll see the changes." And so would she, but he kept that thought to himself.

"Tell me about your family. I know you moved here from San Antonio, but you haven't said much more than that. Do you have any siblings?"

And just like that, tension radiated off of her like steam from a whistling tea kettle. What the heck happened to her that she would tense at just the mention of her family?

Jerry divided his attention between her and the road. She stared straight ahead, but then glanced down at her hands, folded in her lap.

"I have a sister," she finally said, barely above a whisper. "She's two years older, but we're not close. I haven't seen or talked to her in years."

Jerry had so many questions, he didn't know which one to ask first. What he didn't want to do was ask her anything that would have her shutting down completely. But if he didn't ask, it wasn't like she would volunteer any information.

"Do you think you'll ever get married again?" That wasn't the question he had initially intended on asking, but it seemed like a good one to lead with.

"No," she said without hesitation.

"Why not?"

"I can't go through that again."

"Go through what?"

"The lies. The cheating. The betrayal. The blatant disrespect."

With her breakdown in the kitchen earlier, he had assumed that things hadn't been good in her marriage. Now it seemed that they were worse than he initially thought.

"How did your husband die?"

Rayne blew out a long, noisy breath, then propped her elbow on the door and rubbed her forehead. "God, Jerry. Way to go straight to tough questions."

"You know what? Forget I ask. When you're ready to talk about—"

"His lover's husband killed him."

Lover's...husband?

The words jockeyed around in his mind while he processed what she was saying.

"Well...damn, Rayne. I—I, I don't know what to say."

Her humorless laugh drowned out the music floating through the speakers. "Yeah, isn't that some mess? My husband, the man who vowed to love me above all else was screwing around on me. Imagine my surprise when I found out that it was with more than one woman. He ended up hooking up with the wrong woman though."

The more she revealed, the less he knew what to say. He'd been with his share of women, but what he never did were married women. Ever.

"I don't know if he knew the woman was married, but that night he found out the hard way. Her husband walked in on them. He ended up beating Kirk to death with a baseball bat, and seriously injuring his wife...right there in their bed."

"Man, Rayne. I am so sorry."

Jerry exited the highway, and traveled through the streets of downtown, having second thoughts about dinner. Their conversation wasn't the best lead in to a nice, romantic evening. But at least now he had a better understanding about why she was so adamant about not dating him.

"I hate that you went through that."

"Yeah, me too. If only I had known sooner what type of scum I had married. The cheating was bad enough, but I'll never forgive Kirk for the mess he got me into."

Alarm pulsed through Jerry's body. "What type of mess?"

When Rayne didn't respond, Jerry glanced at her. She gnawed on her lower lip then stared out the passenger window. He had a bad feeling this conversation was going to get worse before it got better.

So much for a nice, fun evening.

Chapter Eleven

Rayne wrung her hands, unable to stop fidgeting in her seat. She thought about Kirk often but rarely discussed him and for good reason. Not only would talking about her late husband reveal the type of selfish man she had married, but it would also shine a spotlight on her ignorance at the time.

She sat up straighter when Jerry guided his huge truck into a parking lot of a strip mall.

"Why are we stopping?" she asked when he pulled into a parking spot on the edge of the lot, far from the stores.

He turned off the truck and unsnapped his seatbelt. "Because I want you to talk to me. Tell me what happened."

Rayne blew out a nervous breath. Her friendship with Jerry had been a godsend, but was she ready to open herself up to him? Would he look at her differently? Would he think less of her?

Rayne jumped when Jerry covered her hand with his and brought the back of her fingers to his lips before kissing them. "Just tell me what you want me to know."

"Honestly...I don't know if I want you to know anything about my past. There are some parts I'm not proud of."

"Trust me. We all have things in our pasts that we aren't proud of, but that's the beauty of the past. It's in the past."

He squeezed her hand. "You're here now, building a new life for you and Ladybug. This guy and whatever he did, he can't hurt you anymore."

Thank, God. Rayne had endured about as much as she could handle of Kirk and the mess he left behind.

"I didn't really know my husband." The words spilled out of her mouth in a whoosh, and a quiver of discomfort settled in her gut. Leaving the past in the past wasn't easy when the memories came back in a rush. "I didn't know him as well as I thought I did. Besides the cheating, Kirk had gotten into serious debt. Debt I knew nothing about, but I ended up being responsible for."

"Did he have a gambling problem? Drugs?"

Rayne shook her head. "No. Most of his issues were centered around *women*, but I didn't find out about his betrayal until after he was dead. The day I had to identify his body, was the day my life started unraveling."

Rayne stared down at her and Jerry's joined hands, willing herself not to break down. She had once read that talking about problems or situations out loud gave them less control over your life. Rayne didn't know if that was true. The mental and emotional wounds hadn't healed enough back then, but she was in a different place now. Maybe talking to Jerry would help erase some of the bitterness she'd been carrying for Kirk. Maybe.

"The first two years of our marriage were good, but that last year, year and a half, our relationship slowly deteriorated. No matter how hard I tried to keep our marriage together, nothing helped. And towards the end, I barely saw Kirk. He was either working late or traveling for work, at least that's what he told me."

"How long were you married?"

"A little over three years."

"How did you guys meet?"

Rayne's nerves tensed and she tried drawing strength from Jerry's closeness as her heart rate inched higher. "Foster care."

"So…you grew up in foster care?"

Rayne finally glanced at him. The parking lot lights created shadows across his face, but she didn't miss the concern in his eyes.

"Yes. My mother battled with alcoholism, and my sister and I ended up in the system when I was around six. Mom never got herself together, and neither of us knew our fathers."

Rayne didn't bother telling him that she and her sister had been separated, and hadn't reconnected until they were adults. By then they were strangers. Their sisterly bond hadn't been strong enough to build a relationship.

No. She'd save that conversation for another day.

Rayne hated seeing pity in Jerry's eyes. That was one of many reasons why she rarely shared her past with others. It was difficult to mentally relive those days, as much as it was uncomfortable for people to hear about her beginnings. Her life had been one challenge after another for as long as Rayne could remember, but she survived. She would keep on surviving.

She and Jerry sat in silence until he spoke. "I don't know what to say." Releasing her hand, he cupped her cheek. "I knew early on that you were a tough woman, a survivor of sorts, but I had no idea that…" His words trailed off, and he lowered his hand.

Even if people didn't experience the foster care system first hand, they either knew someone who had, or could imagine what life was like.

"I'm not going to lie, Jerry. It hasn't been easy. Some years have been pure hell, but when I aged out of foster care, I was determined to build a solid life for myself. There were times when I worked two and three jobs, trying to save as much money as I could toward school." There had been programs available to help pay for some of her college expense, but not all of it.

Rayne had vowed to make something of herself and not end up like her mother, who could never get her life together.

Graduating from college and landing a good job was supposed to be Rayne's way out of poverty. This conversation was reminding her of the promise that she made to herself back then, and it didn't matter how long it took, she was going back to school one day.

"At what point did you and Kirk get together?"

"A few years after I graduated from high school. During my teens, I lived in a group home that wasn't too far from the foster home he lived in. After aging out, I didn't see him around but ran into him about six years ago and we started hanging out."

Rayne stared out the windshield as a steady flow of cars pulled into the lot. Most parked close to the stores, leaving them alone on the edge of the parking lot.

"After suffering from abandonment issues and never really allowing anyone to get too close, dating Kirk had been a big step for me. With keeping people at a distance, no one could hurt or leave me again.

"But Kirk...he was everything I wasn't. Fun, charming and with our similar backgrounds, he understood my fears and trust issues. I slowly let my guard down. I let him into my solitary world. We dated a while and eventually got married. At first, things between us were good."

Rayne glanced at Jerry as sadness descended on her.

"He became my everything. It was me and him against the world." Rayne laid her head against the headrest, trying not to let the melancholy consume her. "He was very supportive. I was even able to decrease my work hours to part-time and attend college full time. Then I got pregnant with Stormy, and...everything as I knew it started to change."

"Why? Was he unhappy about the pregnancy?"

"At first he seemed excited. We both were. Considering how we grew up, we had planned to give our child everything we didn't have, and we were going to be present in our baby's life. But months into my pregnancy, Kirk became distant. And after Stormy was born, I saw him even less. But *crazy* me thought he was just working longer hours to better prepare for our future."

"Did you ever question him about his behavior?"

"I did. Kirk's responses were always the same. He was trying to keep money coming in, especially since he encouraged me to focus on finishing that semester of school and staying healthy for our baby."

When she thought back on those latter days, Rayne still couldn't believe how naive she'd been. Thinking back, there had been signs.

"I should've known he was cheating, but I didn't. Or maybe I just didn't want to believe that he would step out on me. It wasn't until after his death that I understood what had been going on."

"Another woman," Jerry said bitterly.

"*Women*. He was financially supporting several women. And worse than that, Kirk and one of his tramps took out loans in my name."

Jerry reared back. "What?"

Rayne nodded. "There was a car purchased in my name, as well as a couple of credit cards."

"They stole your identity?" Shock dripped from his words.

"Yes. I didn't have any credit cards and had paid cash for what little I owned, including my car. I never had a reason to check my credit record, which turned out to be a mistake. Let me tell you. Identity theft is no joke. After Kirk died, I was on my own, trying to raise Stormy and keep a roof over our head. I couldn't afford an attorney at the time. It took me *years* to clear up that mess." Hell, she was still trying to get on solid ground financially.

"Damn, this guy sounds like a real piece of work. Did his life insurance help at all?"

Rayne's pulse pounded in her ears, and the anger that she felt after Kirk's death was back with a vengeance. "Kirk had changed his insurance policy, making another woman the beneficiary."

Jerry's mouth dropped open. "You gotta be fuc…" He shook his head and dropped back against his seat. "If this guy wasn't already dead, I would find him and beat his ass. Who does that kind of shit?"

A humorless laugh burst free from Rayne. "I have asked myself that question a thousand times. I never saw that type of betrayal coming. While we were married, I did everything I could to be a good wife. I never disrespected him, always had dinner on the table when he got home from work, and I always made sure I looked good for him. I don't know what I did to make him deceive me like that."

Jerry leaned forward and reached behind her, cupping the back of her neck. "Baby, I hope you didn't blame yourself for the way he treated you. There was probably nothing you did wrong. Some people are just assholes."

Rayne knew he was right, but that hadn't stopped her from believing that she had done something to deserve that treatment. For years she struggled to forgive herself. Because of her naiveté, Rayne had put her and Stormy in danger by barely being able to provide for them financially. She wanted so bad to give her daughter the life she had dreamed for them.

"There's something I don't understand." Jerry cut into Rayne's thoughts, and she turned to him. "You said that Kirk named someone else as the beneficiary on the life insurance policy. I thought the spouse is automatically the beneficiary."

"In some cases." Rayne swallowed and swiped at a rogue tear that slipped through. "Since Texas is a community property state, I thought the same thing. We both took out policies after we married and by paying the premiums out of our joint account, the policy should've been considered community property. I should've been entitled to at least half of the payout even if I wasn't listed as the beneficiary. But…"

Jerry continued rubbing the back of her neck. "But what?"

"But there was a document on file—a property status document with my signature. It stated that the insurance policy didn't fall under community property and that I waived my rights to any insurance money."

Jerry's brows dipped into a frown. "What made you sign something like that?"

Rayne shook her head, biting down on her bottom lip to keep her emotions in check. "Jerry, I didn't sign that form. Somebody forged my signature. I just couldn't prove it. Even to me, the signature looked identical to mine."

Tears filled her eyes, and she turned, batting them away. She had shed enough tears back then to last a lifetime. No way was she going to cry now.

Without a word, Jerry climbed out of the truck and Rayne watched as he walked around the front of the vehicle. He opened her door and extended his hand.

There was something she saw in his eyes—empathy, compassion, something. It was enough for her not to question him. Instead, she allowed him to help her out of the truck.

"I just want to hug you," he said. "Is that okay?"

Rayne studied him, moved by his words. Her heart opened a little more for him, and she nodded, still feeling a little choked up. "That's always okay."

"Good to know." He pulled her to his body. "I am so sorry for all that you've gone through. No one should have to experience any of that. I'm glad you made it through."

"Because of Stormy. She saved my life," she said against his scented neck. "I had to keep going...to keep fighting...for her."

Rayne didn't know how long she and Jerry stood there, holding each other, but her soul sang with joy as peace settled over her. She had no idea what the future held, but for the first time in a long time, she was looking forward to the possibilities.

Jerry eventually pulled back but didn't release Rayne, placing a feathery kiss on her lips.

"How about if we tweak our plans tonight?"

Rayne narrowed her eyes, especially when he flashed that sexy grin. "Exactly what do you have in mind?"

He glanced down at her feet. "How comfortable are your shoes?"

Her gaze dropped to her four-inch heels. "They're pretty comfortable. Why?"

He smiled and opened the passenger door of his truck. "You'll see."

Chapter Twelve

"I think Dave & Busters is my new favorite place," Rayne said, grinning like a kid in a toy store as they strolled hand in hand through the huge arcade, circling to find another game to play.

God, she was beautiful. This was the first time that he had seen her pretty face perfectly made up and her clothes fit her sexy, curvaceous body as if they had been tailor-made for her. All evening he'd been trying not to focus only on how hot she was looking, but it was hard not to. The woman was *fine* as hell.

During dinner, their conversation flowed easily and Jerry stayed away from personal topics about her past. But he couldn't help staring into those alluring eyes all through their meal as they feasted on bacon cheeseburgers and fries. Each time their gazes met, she captured more of his heart. And all Jerry wanted to do was wipe out the bad memories of her past and replace them with good ones.

Changing their plans and going to Dave & Buster's was the best idea he'd had all day. The fact that Rayne had never been to the restaurant and arcade was an added bonus. But throughout the night, bits and pieces of her past invaded his mind. He had grown up in a loving family, a family he could count on for anything. Finding out she had grown up in foster care gutted him, making him want to hold her and never let her go. He didn't know anyone who grew up without at least one of their parents, and his imagination had gone on a wild ride when she revealed that part of her past.

But what really pissed him the hell off was her late husband. Rayne was one of the sweetest women he'd ever met. To know her asshole of a husband had practically destroyed her life made Jerry want to dig his ass up and kill him all over again. He hated feeling like that, but it was the truth. No one should have to go through what the man put Rayne through.

"I can't remember the last time I played video games, but this has been fun," Rayne shouted over the high volume of game sounds and people talking and laughing.

They had spent the last hour going from one game to another, and it amazed him how good Rayne was at every one she played.

"I'm glad you're having a good time," Jerry said close to her ear. "How are you in basketball? Wanna shoot some hoops?"

She smiled up at him, her light-brown eyes glittering with excitement, and Jerry's heart kicked inside his chest. Damn. He had it bad for this woman. And whether she knew it or not, their relationship had made a turn tonight. Even now, the fact that she was letting him hold her hand spoke volumes. Her guard was slowly lowering, and Jerry had no intention of screwing up the progress he was making with her.

When they made it to Super Shots, one of the basketball games, there were two open bays. They claimed them, barely getting them before two teenage boys walked up.

"I'll go easy on you since you haven't shot hoops in a while," Jerry said.

Rayne waved him off. "Unlike you, who plays basketball every week, it's been a while since I've played, but I can hold my own. Get ready to get whooped by a girl."

Jerry laughed and swiped the power card in the machine to get the game started. "I see you're talking trash now, huh? Well, let me see if you can back up those words."

The game started and they each shot the basketballs quickly, trying to make as many baskets as possible before the time was up. Jerry effortlessly made one basket after another while keeping an eye on Rayne, who indeed was holding her own in between giggles.

When the time was up, Rayne huffed out a breath and leaned over to see his score. He had made almost three times as many baskets as her, but she'd done well.

"Can I play one more time? I was too busy watching you, which threw off my focus. I know I can do better."

"You can play as much as you want."

He stood in front of her bay and swiped the card to get her machine going. Several basketballs rolled toward her.

"I'm not gonna play this time. Then you can't say I distracted you, even though I kinda like knowing that I have that effect on you."

She rolled her eyes, but he didn't miss the smile playing around her enticing lips. "Whatever. Let me show you what I can really do."

Once the time started, Rayne picked up one of the balls, shot it and grabbed another. She was moving faster than before and made the first few baskets effortlessly. By the time the game was over, she had almost doubled her previous score.

"Okay, I'm impressed. If I'd known you could shoot hoops like that, I would've tried harder to get you out on the basketball courts by now," Jerry said.

She huffed out a breath and leaned on the console, visibly winded. "Gosh, that's a lot harder than it looks."

"Well, you made it look easy, baby. I guess you still have some skills from when you were a kid." She once mentioned playing basketball when she was younger and being one of the best players in the neighborhood.

"Yeah, I was kind of a tomboy back then. Loved doing anything that wasn't girlie, from climbing trees to digging up worms. I stayed outside as much as I could."

"Yet, you're raising a girlie-girl who is afraid of spiders and hates getting dirty."

Rayne laughed, something she'd been doing a lot of since they arrived. All Jerry wanted to do was keep that gorgeous smile on her face. As a matter of fact, he was going to make it his mission to do just that. And now that he better understood why she was hesitant to get involved with him, he wasn't giving up on them one day being a couple. He would show her that not all men were like her late husband, and he planned to do whatever it took to win her trust.

Jerry already knew that it wouldn't be easy, especially after their dinner conversation. She blamed herself for everything that happened with Kirk, claiming she should've known the signs and shouldn't have been so trusting. Her biggest regret was that Stormy had to endure the drama right along with her after Kirk's death. Even though her daughter showed no signs of being traumatized, Rayne was afraid of what Stormy might remember during those few years.

Jerry didn't care how long it took. He would wait for Rayne. He already knew she was worth it, and more than anything, she deserved a happily ever after and he wanted to be the man to give it to her.

Good thing he was a patient man, and if he played his cards right, his patience would pay off.

*

Rayne followed behind Jerry as he carried Stormy up the stairs to her bedroom. She didn't know what all her child had done over Mr. and Mrs. Jenkins' house, but whatever it was had worn Stormy out. She hadn't stirred during the trip home. Rayne already knew that her little talker was going to have a lot to tell her in the morning.

Once they tucked Stormy into bed, Rayne kissed her daughter before they silently left the room.

"I've heard my cousins talk about their kids climbing into bed with them in the middle of the night. Does Stormy do that?" Jerry asked as they walked back down the stairs.

"Not since we moved here. We used to have to share a bedroom. Now that Stormy has her own room, she rarely sleeps with me unless there's a storm. On those nights, she's quick to climb into my bed."

Jerry nodded, and Rayne felt even more grateful for their current home. There had been plenty of times when their living quarters hadn't been the best. Times when she'd been afraid to close her eyes for fear they weren't in a safe environment. But she had done the best she could with her limited funds, and it was by the grace of God that they'd survived.

She strolled into the kitchen and washed her hands in the sink. "Want something to drink?"

"Water would be good."

Grabbing the water pitcher from the refrigerator, Rayne poured them both a glass. "Tonight, was fun," she said.

"I agree, and I'm glad you had a good time. Does that mean you'll consider going out with me again…and again after that?" He flashed that sexy grin that sent heat rushing through her body.

Smiling, Rayne shook her head. She didn't dare tell him that the thought had popped into her head on the way to his parents' house. Even though she knew it was just fear keeping her from dating anyone, she still couldn't seem to get past her experience with Kirk. But what she did know, was Jerry was nothing like him. He was a good man, and Rayne was lucky to have him in her life…even as a friend.

"I don't think you should wait on me, Jerry. Find someone you can have a future with."

"That someone is you."

"That someone needs to be a person who wants to get married. Someone who can make you happy, because I already know you're going to be a wonderful husband." Those words left Rayne's mouth dry. The thought of him with another woman made her stomach hurt, but she was still too damaged for a relationship...and scared.

Jerry gulped half the contents of his glass before setting it on the counter. "That someone could be you."

"We're not doing this back and forth dance tonight," she said, a little disappointed in herself. Here she had this great guy who wanted to get to know her even better, and she was pushing him away, again.

Jerry brushed the back of his fingers down Rayne's cheek, and her skin tingled from the contact. "I thought you wanted a family."

"I do...I did," she added quickly. "Actually, I have a family—Stormy."

Rayne lowered her eyes and stared down at the floor, but felt the heat of his gaze. Her desire to have a big family hadn't diminished. She just couldn't see herself getting married again. Trusting had never come easy, and after Kirk's deception, Rayne had vowed never to rely on a man again. But she'd be lying if she said that Jerry didn't tempt her to do just that. Spending time with him, she'd felt special, treasured. Feelings she hadn't experienced in years, if ever.

He tilted her chin, forcing her to look at him, and their eyes locked on each other. He really was a gorgeous man with smooth, dark skin and those penetrating eyes that Rayne could easily get lost in.

But then her eyes dropped to his full, kissable lips, and she swallowed hard. She had told herself that their outing tonight wasn't a real date. It was just two friends hanging out and celebrating his birthday, but she really wouldn't mind kissing her *friend* again.

"You're right," he said. "Stormy is your family, but don't you want to build upon that family? What happens when she goes off to college? I'm sure you're not going to want to spend your life alone."

Her daughter going off to college was the last thing Rayne wanted to think about right now. She had cried like a baby the first time she'd taken Stormy to pre-K. Had it not been for the teacher who insisted that they'd take very good care of her daughter, Rayne would've walked back out of the building with her child.

And then there was Stormy. The moment she saw the other children in the classroom, she left Rayne at the door and walked into the room like a boss. All Rayne could do was look on as her daughter started introducing herself to her classmates.

Rayne smiled at the memory, but it slipped when she thought about what Jerry said. *College*. She would never want to hold her little girl back from doing something she wanted to do, but it wouldn't be easy to let her go.

"How do you know she'll want to go to college?" Rayne asked, moving to her right to put some distance between her and Jerry. Between the enticing scent of his cologne and the intense desire to kiss him, they were a little too close for comfort.

"I have no doubt that Ladybug is going to college. She's too outgoing and sociable not to want that type of experience. And hell, as intelligent as she is, she's going one day even if I have to pay for it myself," he said with conviction. Rayne grinned, loving how much he cared about her child. "I predict that she'll major in something centered around caring for people like pre-med or maybe she'll attend nursing school or become a psychiatrist."

"Hmm…interesting you should say that. I majored in psychology during my two years of college. Well, almost two years."

"I didn't know that."

Rayne carried her glass of water to the table and sat down. Jerry claimed the chair next to her.

"Yeah, after I had Stormy, I stopped going to school but intended to go back when she was older. And after Kirk died, I couldn't keep up mentally or financially." With her finger, Rayne wiped some of the condensation from the side of the glass. "I was so lost. I hadn't realized just how dependent on him I had become. I wanted to give up, but I couldn't.

Stormy was counting on me, and I knew I had to get myself together for her sake. All I kept thinking was that I didn't want her to grow up in foster care like I had. I couldn't let her down the way my parents had done to me."

Jerry rubbed her back in a slow, soothing motion. "I'm so glad you didn't give up. Otherwise, I wouldn't have the pleasure of having you and Ladybug in my life."

That was one of the sweetest things anyone had ever said to her. Rayne studied his profile as he stared down at the table, lost in thought. She prayed that their friendship continued to blossom despite the anxiety creeping in at the thought of them getting closer. It had been easier to fight the attraction before they had kissed. Now, after spending quality time with him, Rayne longed to get to know him better.

But fear was a powerful emotion.

She had been abandoned one too many times in her life, and Rayne didn't know if she could survive that type of heartache again. Yet, she had a feeling that anything she experienced with Jerry would be different...better. But still...

"Do you think you'll ever go back and finish your degree?"

"I'd love to, but I'm still trying to...I'm still trying to create a stable life for me and Stormy. One day, though, I'll finish my education."

"I think you should. Let me know if there's anything I can do to make that a reality."

Rayne nodded. He was always offering to help her in one way or the other, which she wasn't used to, at least not since before she and Kirk had married. But either way, that was one goal she planned to accomplish.

Then I can get a better job and give Stormy the type of life I always dreamed for us.

That was her number one goal—to give her daughter a better life than she had.

Jerry glanced at his watch. "It's late. I'd better let you get to bed."

Rayne wasn't ready for the night to end, but instead of telling him that, she followed him to the door.

Jerry stopped and turned. "I understand being afraid to trust again. I just hope you remember that I'm not *him*."

When he placed his hand on her hip, urging her closer, Rayne went willingly. Her defenses were no match for this man. They were getting weaker by the minute, especially when he looked at her with concern in his eyes. He was slowly chipping away at that wall of defense that she had carefully constructed around her heart.

"I think it was fate that you moved in next door to me. This attraction vibing between us is something I have never felt with anyone. *Ever.* But now that I know what you've been through, I don't blame you for being hesitant to get involved with someone again." He cupped her cheek, brushing the pad of his thumb over her skin as he continued to stare into her eyes. "Just know that when—"

Rayne placed her finger on his lips. "I know."

Jerry had been a lifeline for her. A lifeline that she had desperately needed when they first moved to town. Since then, he had become someone she could truly count on. And someone she was seriously attracted to.

Then why am I afraid to take a chance on him...on us?

An overwhelming desire to kiss him forced Rayne closer, and without second-guessing herself, she snaked her arms around Jerry's neck and covered his mouth with hers. She put everything she felt for him in the kiss as desire pulsed through her body, and he matched her stroke for stroke.

She might've started the kiss, but Jerry quickly took charge, tightening the hold he had around her waist backing her against the front door. Heat rippled under her skin as the flush of sexual desire, that she hadn't felt in years, consumed her.

Heaven.

That's what it felt like being in his strong arms.

Pure heaven.

Jerry expertly freed the hairpins from her hair and ran his fingers through her tresses.

God, that's sexy, she thought, enjoying the feel of his hands against her scalp.

"I love your hair," he said against her lips, then held her head in place as he continued devouring her mouth.

The kiss was urgent, yet exploratory, and she was no longer surprised by the way her body responded to him. They'd had a connection from day one, and she was so tired of denying herself.

Rayne arched into him, loving the feel of being hugged up against his muscular body. If she didn't know how much he desired her before, she knew now. His erection pressed against her stomach as their hunger for each other grew. And with every powerful thrust of his tongue, she wanted him that much more.

Rayne was panting when they finally came up for air. She wasn't alone. Jerry pressed his forehead to hers, breathing just as hard.

"I love kissing you, but I'd better leave now before I go too far." He straightened to his full height and started to move away.

"I changed my mind," Rayne blurted, surprising even herself.

Jerry froze, then his left brow lifted in question, but he said nothing.

With her heart pounding hard against her rib cage, she could barely think straight. A mixture of excitement and fear consumed her. "Maybe we can um...hang out a little more often."

A slow, sexy smile tugged up the corner of Jerry's mouth, and Rayne's pulse thumped a little faster.

"You mean like...we can *officially* start dating? Because if that's what you're saying, I want it clear that you're mine," he said with authority, reclaiming his spot right in front of her. "I don't want there to be any misunderstanding about that. So is that what you're saying?"

Rayne lowered her gaze and bit her bottom lip. What was she doing? Was she ready for a commitment? What about his playboy past? Hell, what about her past? Could she really trust a man again? Would she end up worse off than she'd been before if this relationship ended badly?

Just moments ago, she was still fighting her feelings. How could a kiss make her change her mind that quickly?

"Hey. Look at me," Jerry insisted, and Rayne met his gaze. "I know you're scared, but baby I'm not going to hurt you. Give me a chance to prove to you that I'm *not* Kirk

Rayne knew he wouldn't intentionally hurt her, but it was the unintentional harm that he could do that concerned her. What she felt for him was stronger than she'd felt about anyone in a long time and that scared her to death. But if Rayne didn't leap…if she didn't take a chance and open her heart, she might miss out on the best thing that ever happened to her outside of giving birth to Stormy.

"So, what do you say? Wanna be my woman?" he asked, his baritone deeper than usual.

"Yes," she responded more breathily than intended. Before Rayne could form her next thought, Jerry kissed her. The slow, drugging kiss was even more intense than the previous one, and her worries melted away. They were replaced with an excitement Rayne hadn't felt before tonight.

When the kiss ended, Jerry brushed long strands of hair away from her face. "I'll let you set the pace in our relationship. As long as you're mine, we can take things as slow as you want."

Rayne nodded. "Okay."

The saying, *this is the first day of the rest of your life,* came to mind, and she couldn't wait to see what came next.

Chapter Thirteen

Rayne moaned. Her hammering heart beating double-time like the wings of a hummingbird as Jerry hovered above her, sending tingles of delight pulsing through her body. The mere touch of his lips on her heated skin, tracing a path down her neck and between the valley of her breasts, while he thrust in and out of her, had Rayne on the edge of her release.

"Jerry," she panted, unable to finish a complete thought with him moving inside of her. She gripped his perfectly firm butt and rocked her hips in tune to the pace he had set. She knew they'd be good together, but the way he made her body hum exceeded anything she could have imagined.

"Oh," she whimpered, and her eyes slammed shut as ripples of pleasure consumed her.

Jerry slid in and out of her tightness with more force, his momentum picking up with each thrust of his hips. This was their second round and it was even more intense than the first, and Rayne knew she couldn't hold on much longer.

But when he slowed, her eyes flew open. "Don't stop. Please don't stop," she begged, her breathing ragged as her body vibrated, wound tight enough to snap.

A sly smile lifted the right corner of Jerry's mouth before he lowered his head. "I can't get enough of you," he crooned, his words smothered on her breast.

Rayne would never get enough of him either, especially with the way his tongue swirled around her sensitive nipple before he pulled the hardened peak between his lips. Licking, sucking, with each lap of his tongue, he drove into her deeper and harder, gradually picking up speed.

Jerry lifted his head, and her nipple popped from his mouth. "Damn you feel good," he moaned. With one hand gripping the headboard, he lifted her left hip off the bed and drove into her like he was on automatic pilot.

Oh yeah, that's it. She fisted the sheet as he drove in and out of her. He was the one who felt good, his thick shaft filling her completely.

His fingers tightened on the back of her thigh, and he moved faster, their heavy breathing filling the room.

"J—Jerry," Rayne stuttered, barely able to breathe, an orgasm teetered on the edge of her control.

"Come for me, baby," he said through gritted teeth, moving frantically as if he too was on the brink of his release.

"I-I..." Rayne's words stalled in her throat and her senses short-circuited as a massive orgasm rushed through her body. "Jerry!"

Rayne jerked awake, her pulse pounding in her ears as she scrambled into a sitting position in her bed. With her chest heaving, she glanced anxiously around the dimly lit bedroom, taking in the sparsely furnished space. The only sound was that of the ticking alarm clock sitting on the bedside table.

Her gaze dropped to her damp tank top and the shorts she was sleeping in, as well as the disheveled bedding. But there was no Jerry.

Crap. It was only a dream.

Rayne loosened the grip on the bed-sheet balled in her hand and brought her knees to her chest, squeezing her thighs together to tap down the sensuous throb at her core. The dream had seemed so real...so intimate...so *hot*.

She released a frustrated sigh and covered her face with her hands as her body continued to pulse. Disappointment lodged in her throat.

Good, Lord. If dreaming about him got her that worked up, what would happen if...or when they finally came together? Rayne hadn't had sex in years, and for the first time in a long time, her body vibrated with sexual energy. The foreign feeling was exciting and disappointing at the same time.

As a single mom, with no immediate family to babysit, getting laid hadn't been an option. But even if the opportunity had presented itself, Rayne wouldn't have been interested. All that Kirk had done to her had ruined her desire to get with another man.

Until now.

But it had just been a dream. A fantasy. Would she ever have the pleasure of experiencing that type of heated passion? And if she ever did, she only wanted one person.

Jerry Jenkins.

Rayne threw back the covers, left the bedroom, and headed to the bathroom. She was too sticky from perspiration to fall back to sleep.

After a quick, cold, shower, she slipped into a pair of pajamas and returned to her bedroom. Climbing back into bed, she felt refreshed but still a little wired.

The night before, Jerry had told her they could go as slow as she wanted, but now she was tempted to call him. She didn't want to go slow. If there was a chance that dream could become a reality, Rayne wanted to go for it.

But she couldn't.

There was no way she would have sex with anyone, not even Jerry, while her daughter was in the house. How the heck were they going to *date* and keep everything rated G with Stormy around?

Rayne huffed out a breath and snuggled deeper into her pillow, but as soon as she closed her eyes, her cell phone vibrated on the table next to the bed. She grabbed the device and glanced at the bright screen.

Charlee.

"Hello," she answered.

"Rise and shine, sleepy head. How was your date? Is Tall, Dark, and Handsome in bed with you?" her friend asked, humor in her voice.

"Ha! I wish." The words slipped through her lips before Rayne could pull them back. She hadn't intended to share that thought out loud.

"Hold the heck up. Is that disappointment I hear in your voice? Are you saying that you wanted to get a little something, something going last night and that dark chocolate hunk didn't stay?"

Rayne sighed, but then a slow smile spread across her mouth, knowing her friend was about to freak when Rayne told her the news.

"Girl, you better say something." Charlee's tone grew louder with each word.

"Let's just say, Jerry and I are officially dating."

"Get the hell out of here! Are you kidding me?" Charlee screamed, and Rayne pulled the phone from her ear, laughing. "I don't believe you. What happened to *I'm not ready to date. He's just a friend* and all that other crap you were spewing?"

"I—I, I didn't think I was ready, but last night, something changed between us." Or at least, something had changed within her.

"Well, damn. What did Jerry do, get between those thighs of yours and give you some tongue action? Because I know you. He had to put it down *real* good to make you change your mind like that."

"It wasn't like that," Rayne said quietly, searching her brain trying to determine exactly what happened to change her mind. All she could recall was the intense need to spend more time with him and the peace that surrounded her while in his presence.

"Then exactly how was it? He had to do something to make you do a one-eighty like that."

"He's just…an amazing man," Rayne said wistfully. She told her friend about the evening, getting a little misty as she thought about how sweet Jerry had been. Though she'd been looking forward to going to the fancy restaurant, Dave & Busters had been a better choice. She needed to relax and laugh some, something she hadn't been doing enough of.

Charlee remained silent, listening as Rayne told her about the conversation and the kiss that led up to her decision.

"You didn't wake up with a change of heart, did you?"

No way would she tell her friend how she woke up.

"No. Even though I don't think Jerry would ever treat me the way Kirk did, I'm going into this relationship with my eyes wide open. I learned my lesson with Kirk. No man will ever get a chance to make a fool of me again."

"Well, I'm glad you're giving Jerry a chance. I'm pulling for you guys. You deserve some happiness and some *hot* sex, and I think Jerry's just the man for the job."

"Apparently, you have forgotten about your goddaughter. I have no idea how to date with a child."

Rayne had only met a few single moms since moving to town and none that she would take advise from. She wasn't a prude, at least she didn't think she was, but the way a couple of the women carried themselves at work told her that anything went when it came to dating. They had a couple of children each, but most of their conversations centered around what they wore to the club and the men they hooked up with.

"I'm sure you and Jerry will figure it out. Besides, I'll babysit whenever I'm in town."

"But you're never in town."

Charlee sighed. She once loved her job and the travel, but lately Rayne sensed that her friend wasn't as into either as she used to be.

"That might be changing soon," Charlee finally said. "I have a meeting with my father and a couple of his advisers in a few weeks. I'm thinking about cutting down on the travel, but I'm still working on a plan on how that will work."

"That would be great. I would love for us to hang out more, which reminds me. What was that all about with you and Liam?"

The silence through the phone line was thicker than a concrete block, making Rayne even more curious.

"Charlee, you know my deepest darkest secrets. There's no way whatever happened between you and Liam can be any worse than what I've been through."

"No, it's not. Liam and I were...together for a while before I messed up."

"What happened, and why haven't you ever mentioned him?"

"He and I were an item before you moved to town."

"But we've talked about the Jenkins family. You had plenty of opportunity to tell me about you two."

"I know. I guess I've been trying to forget and move on."

"But it sounds like you haven't. Do you still care about Liam?"

"Yes. Always. He was the best thing that ever happened to me, but I hurt him. I'm surprised he even said anything to me yesterday."

"I take it you guys haven't seen each other in a while."

"Not since the day we broke up. Almost a year ago."

Rayne had never heard her friend sound so down. Charlee was like Stormy. An extrovert who loved life and people. Rarely was she ever down about anything.

"I hear he's single," Rayne said. During dinner the night before, Jerry had mentioned that his cousin wasn't dating anyone as far as he knew.

Charlee released a harsh laugh. "Trust me. I'm the last person he would ever get with, and I don't blame him. I don't deserve him."

Rayne tsked. "Don't say that. He'd be lucky to have you. Maybe—"

"Rayne, I appreciate what you're trying to do, but Liam and I are history. And on that note, I'd better get off this phone. I'm using today to work on a couple of upcoming presentations."

"So how is Chicago?" Rayne asked, understanding her friend's need to change the subject. One day when they were in the same city, she planned to revisit the conversation.

"You know how much I love Chicago. It's wonderful. I'll be here a few days, and then I'll be heading to Detroit."

They talked for a few more minutes before disconnecting. Rayne glanced at the time. *Seven-thirty-five.* If she was lucky, she might be able to get a little sleep before Stormy woke up.

She reached over to set her phone on the nightstand.

"Mommy! Mommy!"

Rayne jumped and dropped her phone, ignoring it as it landed with a thud on the carpet. "Stormy, I'm in here," she said, struggling to free herself from the covers so she could find out what was wrong. Stormy only screamed like that if she was hurt or excited.

By the time Rayne untangled herself from the bedding and stood, Stormy tore into the room.

"Mommy, I'm rich! I'm rich," she screamed, waving her arms in the air with something in her hands. "Look. Look, I got two dollars."

Rayne looked at the two five-dollar bills and frowned. "Stormy, this is ten-dollars. Where'd you get this from?"

"The tooth fairy. She put it under my pillow!" She jumped up and down with the energy of a person who had consumed a pound of sugar. "Did I get more than Anna?"

Rayne groaned. On the one hand, she could kiss Jerry for remembering to play tooth fairy. He must've slipped the money under the pillow when he laid Stormy down the night before. On the other hand, her child was going to expect the tooth fairy and money with every tooth she loss.

Rayne shook the thoughts free and focused on her daughter.

"This is a lot of money. What are you going to do with it?" she asked, not bothering to answer the question about Anna. The last thing Rayne wanted was for Stormy to start bragging to the little girl about how much money she received.

They both climbed onto the bed and sat with their backs against the headboard. Stormy looped her arm through Rayne's. God, she loved this little girl.

"I'm going to buy me and you some ice cream because ice cream makes us happy." Stormy beamed and Rayne couldn't help but smile. This child made her heart sing and was her everything. Rayne couldn't imagine her life without her.

"That's so sweet, honey, but wouldn't you rather buy a book?"

A crease formed on Stormy's forehead as she pondered the question. "Do I have enough to buy both?"

"Maybe if we buy ice cream from the grocery store. Then you might have enough. If not, I might have a few dollars to add to what you have."

"Yay!" Stormy cheered, raising her arms and waving the money around. "Can I call Jerry so I can tell him?"

Rayne knew that was coming. "It's too early. Now tell me what you did at Mr. & Mrs. Jenkins' house. Was it fun over there?"

The excitement in her eyes grew more intense. "It was awesome!"

Rayne laughed. Seemed her daughter learned a new word every day, but she couldn't remember her using *awesome*. No doubt she'd be using it every chance she got.

For the next half an hour, Rayne listened as Stormy explained the Jenkins' family movie night. Pizza, home-baked cookies, a Disney movie, popcorn, and Mr. Jenkins teaching her how to play *Go Fish* were the highlights.

Rayne's heart swelled. Hearing how happy Jerry's parents had made her little girl meant everything. There had been so many days when she questioned the decision to move to Cincinnati, but now it felt as if they were right where they were supposed to be.

Chapter Fourteen

Jerry grabbed a beer out of his refrigerator and turned, but stopped abruptly. Rayne was sitting at his breakfast bar staring at him. *Again.*

"Why are you looking at me like that?"

Her brows shot up, and he almost laughed at the startled surprise on her gorgeous face. She had been checking him out on a sly and then zoning out for the last two hours, ever since she and Stormy came over for dinner.

She had also been quieter than usual. Not that Rayne was a big talker, but usually when they hung out, conversation flowed steadily. Not today. Today, she seemed deep in thought. He hoped she wasn't having second thoughts about them. Last night she had shocked the heck out of him when she agreed to be his woman, and Jerry was excited about their future together.

"Looking at you like what?" Rayne finally asked, her attention on his laptop screen that was sitting in front of her. After dinner, she had asked to use the computer to search for jobs.

Jerry walked around the breakfast bar and leaned on the counter. He kept his voice low when he said, "Looking at me like you want to rip my clothes off and have your way with my body."

With her fair skin, he couldn't miss the blush coloring her cheeks. She bit down on her lower lip but didn't say anything.

Hmm… Okay, so he hadn't imagined the lust in her eyes earlier. She wanted him as bad as he wanted her. But what Jerry wasn't going to do was push Rayne into doing something she might not be ready for. He'd been serious the night before about them taking things slow. Even if it meant having to keep giving himself a hand job in the shower every day, he'd do it.

Last night had been a true test, though. He had tossed and turned with her on his mind, and had been tempted to go back to her place and pick up where they'd left off. He had gotten a little carried away. One of their heated kisses had gotten out of control before he left. He had pinned her to the front door, kissing her senseless and caressing her luscious body.

Rayne was a temptation he was finding hard to resist. Even now, he wanted to take her upstairs to his bedroom and make mad, passionate love to her. Or hell, taking her right there up against the counter would work too.

But they couldn't take advantage of either of those options. Stormy might not be paying them any attention, but she was in the family room. With the open concept floorplan, they could see her and vice versa. They had to be careful of what they said and did in front of her.

Rayne turned to him, one arched brow lifted. "Now, who's staring? Why are *you* looking at me like that?"

Jerry leaned in close, inhaling her fresh scent as he put a lingering kiss on her neck. "I want to lick every inch of your body, and then sex you up so good, you won't be able to walk straight for days."

Her mouth dropped open, then closed and opened again, but no words came out.

"Now, are you going to tell me why you've been acting strange since walking into my place?"

Her gaze dropped to his lips before returning to his eyes. "I want you so damn bad. I even dreamed that you screwed my brains out last night," she whispered. "I woke up in a cold sweat, screaming your name, and now all I can think about is your hot, naked body joined with mine."

Now he was the one staring at her with wide eyes and doing the guppy thing with his mouth. How the hell was he going to take it slow knowing she was having those types of dreams? But hearing her speak those words to him, especially considering how reserved she usually was, had Jerry ready to strip her naked and turn her dream into a reality. Consequences be damned.

But that was the old Jerry. He had to be smarter with Rayne. She was it for him. He didn't see a future with anyone else but her, and he didn't want to mess this up with a quick lay. Besides, it wasn't just them they had to think about.

He glanced back at Stormy, who was still engrossed in the video game, then turned to Rayne. Unable to resist any longer, he covered her mouth with his. Each kiss between them got sweeter and sweeter, and when her lips parted slightly, he slid his tongue in and savored her goodness.

He had only intended the kiss to be brief, but Rayne fisted the front of his shirt, pulling him closer. His hand went automatically to the small of her back, and he held on. Jerry didn't know what had gotten into her, but whatever it was, he liked this assertive side of her. And sneaking in a kiss here and there only added to their new adventure.

But as reality set in, Jerry loosened his hold on her. They hadn't discussed how they would behave in front of Stormy, and until they did, he didn't want to get caught making love to Rayne's mouth.

"Were we as good together as I know we'll be?" Jerry asked when they pulled apart, still thinking about her dream.

Rayne swallowed, her eyes as dazed as he felt. They were going to burn up the sheets whenever he did finally get her into his bed.

She swiped her tongue across her bottom lip, making him want to kiss her again.

"Well, were we?" he prodded.

"I just told you I woke up screaming your name. What do you think?"

His dick twitched, wanting so bad to be buried deep inside of her. But Jerry kept that thought to himself.

"I think I'm going to have to put some babysitters on speed dial."

Rayne laughed and returned her attention to the computer screen.

But Jerry was serious. There were several people in his family he could get to look after Stormy if needed. The only thing stopping him from dialing his parents right now, was that he wasn't ready for him and Rayne to jump into bed, yet. This wasn't one of his hit-it and quit-it flings. He planned to prove to her that he was serious about them being together for the long haul.

Jerry adjusted himself, his semi-erection pressing hard against his zipper. He grabbed his beer and took a long drag of the cold brew before setting the bottle on the bar. For the last few months, his will-power had definitely been tested. He hadn't gone this long without sex since he was seventeen, and who knew how much longer he'd have to go without.

In the end, it will all be worth it, he thought.

"How's the search going?" he asked. Rayne had mentioned the other day that she wanted to find either another job that paid more or some part-time work.

"A little slow." She twirled a long strand of her hair around her finger, dividing her attention between him and the screen. "So many of these jobs require a college degree."

"What type of work are you looking for?"

"I wouldn't mind office work, but that would mean office hours. I have to have something flexible that I can work around Stormy's school hours, and be able to take off at a moment's notice. I don't know if I'd get that flexibility with an office job."

"Well, keep in mind that you have a lot more support now with me and my family. All you have to do is let us know when or if we're needed to help you out. Don't worry so much about the work hours, find something that you'll enjoy doing. Then we'll figure out the rest."

She cocked a brow. "We?"

"Yeah, *we*." Jerry draped his arm around her shoulders. "That's one of the perks of being my woman. You have me to bounce thoughts and ideas off of, and someone you can count on." And once she got to know some of his cousins, she'd eventually find out the advantages of being a part of a large family.

Jerry finished off his beer and stood. "Also, while you're on the computer, pull together a resumé. I'll see if we have any openings at J & S. And I can pass it along to some of my family members who have their own businesses or might know of some other available positions."

"Jerry, I can't ask you to do that. Our relationship is new. What if things don't work out between us? It could get awkward working for—"

"First of all, you didn't ask me to do this, but I want to. Secondly, you and I will be together forever. Even if things don't work out, which I believe they will, we'll always be friends. Besides, the best jobs are found through connections, and the Jenkins family is well connected."

She fiddled with the ink pen that was sitting next to the laptop. Jerry could almost hear the wheels in her head turning. She was a proud woman, and now that he knew about her past, he understood why it was so hard for her to ask for help. Until moving to Cincinnati, she had no one.

"You're not alone anymore, Rayne. I'm here for you, okay?"

She swallowed and nodded. "Thank you. I appreciate that."

Jerry didn't know how long it would take for her to fully understand the lengths that he would go for her. Until she did, he'd just have to keep showing her.

Chapter Fifteen

"Bye, Mommy," Stormy said in a sing-song voice before she hurried into the classroom to join her friends.

"She is such a sweetheart and so smart," Mrs. St. John, Stormy's daycare teacher, said. "Yesterday, I caught her helping one of her classmates with his ABCs, and I laughed to myself at how she sounded so much like me. I can already tell she's a leader and a nurturer.

Rayne glanced across the room and found Stormy in the kitchen play area with two other little girls. "She loves people, especially other kids."

Mrs. St. John nodded. "I can tell. She's quick to comfort them, like the other day when another child accidentally ripped her art project. Stormy helped her fix it and then hugged her. It was the cutest scene. You have yourself a special little girl."

Rayne smiled, proud of herself and her daughter. "Thank you."

During Stormy's first years of life, Rayne had been so afraid that she would fail her child the way her mother had failed her. She had overcompensated in every area out of fear, almost driving herself crazy trying to be the perfect mommy. After Kirk's death, all that changed. She fell apart, nearly ruining her and her child's life. It took a while to get herself together, and to this day, she prayed that the drama they endured had no long-term adverse effect on her child.

After saying goodbye to Mrs. St. John, Rayne pulled her cell phone from her handbag to check the time and then headed to her car. She still had another hour before she had to be at work. She could make a couple of stops, including getting some gas, with a few minutes to spare.

She climbed into her old Chevy and set the cell phone in the cup holder. Pulling out of the parking lot, thoughts of Jerry invaded her mind. A flutter of excitement swirled inside her gut. The last seven weeks with him had been some of the best weeks of her life. Rayne couldn't ever remember feeling so alive, so happy, so invigorated. She had been cautiously optimistic when they first started dating, but now she wanted to spend every waking hour with the man.

It was still early in their relationship, but so far Jerry was the perfect boyfriend. Funny, respectful, thoughtful, and the sexiest man alive.

"Whew!" Rayne fanned herself, then laughed at the giddiness bubbling inside of her. She was behaving like a high schooler, crushing on the cutest boy in class. But who wouldn't? Jerry was the total package. Just thinking about him made her all hot and excited.

As she stopped at a traffic light, her cell phone rang. A smile spread across her face before she hit the speaker button.

"I was just thinking about you," she greeted.

"Hey, beautiful. How you doin' this morning?" Jerry's deep baritone filled the car and washed over Rayne like a ray of sunlight on a cloudless day. Even his voice turned her on these days.

"Now that I've heard your sexy voice, I'm great." Rayne had never been a flirt, or talked sexy, but with Jerry, some of the stuff that came out of her mouth surprised even her.

He chuckled. "I feel the same way. Is everything all set for Stormy tonight?" he asked.

"Yup. I talked with your mom. She and your dad are going to pick up Stormy from my place by six-fifteen."

Rayne adored Jerry's parents, especially his mom. Violet was as beautiful on the inside as she was on the outside, and they had developed a wonderful relationship. Growing up in foster care, Rayne had only had one foster mother who seemed to really care about her, but no one like that in her adult life. Spending time with Violet was a welcomed change.

Jerry's parents had also become their go-to babysitters, but Rayne tried not to take advantage of their kindness. Besides, Stormy was her responsibility. It didn't seem right putting her child off on someone else. But tonight, she planned to have some alone time with her man.

"In about nine hours or so, I'll be all yours," she said to Jerry.

"And, baby, I'm counting down the minutes," he crooned. "I can't wait to have you all to myself."

Tonight, would be another turning point in their relationship. Despite the sexual tension growing almost unbearable between them, and their heavy petting sessions reaching explosive levels, they hadn't consummated their relationship. They'd had some close calls, but were both always mindful of Stormy.

Shortly after they started dating, Rayne had told Stormy that Jerry was her boyfriend. She wasn't sure how much her daughter understood, but Stormy loved that the three of them were spending a lot of time together.

"We have dinner reservations for seven, and then we'll head to the hotel," Jerry explained.

Rayne gripped the steering wheel and did a happy dance in her seat. She could count on one hand, with fingers left over, how many times she had stayed at a hotel. Not only was she looking forward to a little R&R, but more than that, she was ready for her and Jerry to take their relationship to the next level.

"But, Rayne, I need to know. Are you sure about tonight? We don't have to—"

"I'm positive. I want this as much as you do. I know it hasn't been easy dating a single mom."

"Having you and Stormy in my life has been a gift. I've loved every minute of our time together, but I ain't gonna lie. I can't wait to get your *fine* ass into bed."

Rayne was cheesing so hard, anyone peeking into her car would think something was wrong with her. Something was—she was falling hard for Jerry Jenkins and could barely contain her excitement. Heck, Rayne didn't want to contain it. Instead, she wanted to scream it to the world that she was falling in love with an amazing man.

"All right, babe. I need to get back to work. Hit me up on my cell during your lunch break."

"Will do." Rayne disconnected the call, thinking about how they had gotten into such a comfortable routine. They talked at least two times during the day, saw each other every evening, and spent most of their weekends together. This man had definitely worked his way into her heart, and she could barely remember how her life was before they started dating.

A car horn blew, and Rayne glanced in the rearview mirror before realizing the traffic light had turned green. The person behind her blew again.

"All right, all right, I'm going. Geez. Be patient."

She drove another block before turning into a gas station and pulling up next to one of the pumps. Just as she turned off the car, her cell phone rang again. She thought it was Jerry calling back until she picked up the device and saw the screen, recognizing her work number.

"Hi, this is Rayne."

"Hey, Rayne. I'm glad I caught you." Sandra Collier's soft voice didn't match her appearance. She was almost six feet tall and about Rayne's size, but her voice sounded like that of a seven-year-old. She was one of the nicest people, but whenever she talked, it was hard to take her seriously.

"What's going on?" Rayne asked, hoping she didn't have to work late. She didn't want anything to delay her plans with Jerry.

"I hate calling you like this, but I wanted to catch you before you came in." Sandra's voice drifted into a hushed whisper, setting off warning bells inside of Rayne. "Management has been doing some reorganizing, and unfortunately, we're going to have to lay you off."

Dread spread through Rayne's body. "What?" She heard her supervisor clearly, but couldn't wrap her brain around how this could be happening.

She sat stunned, barely listening as Sandra continued her speech about model employee, downsizing, seniority, layoffs, and a final check. By the time her supervisor was finished, Rayne's head was spinning.

"I—I can't believe..." Rayne's voice cracked. She had started looking for another job, but so far, nothing had materialized. The factory didn't pay much, but at least it was keeping a roof over their head and food on the table. She needed this job.

A couple of weeks ago, she had finally given her skimpy resumé to Jerry, embarrassed that she didn't have much education or experience. So far, it hadn't attracted anyone enough to give her an interview, but she'd been hopeful. But now...

Thoughts of her financial responsibilities flashed through her mind. She also thought about Stormy and the daycare center they both loved. Without a job, Rayne wouldn't get the childcare subsidy, and she couldn't afford to pay out of pocket.

Her chest tightened as anxiety clawed through her body. Every time her life seemed as if it was on the right track, something happened to knock her back on her ass. She couldn't catch a break.

"I'm so sorry, Rayne."

"I can't believe you're laying me off and with a phone call at that," she snapped. "You could've at least had the decency to tell me face to face."

"Rayne...I'm sorry. I'm just following protocol. This is not personal. You've been a good employee over the last few months, but unfortunately, cuts had to be made."

Long after the call ended, Rayne sat numbly with the phone pressed to her ear. She had no idea what she was going to do.

Laughing outside caught her attention. Two women, dressed in office attire and carrying coffee cups, talked animatedly as they walk to a shiny red BMW. Rayne stared long after they drove off, wondering when it would be her turn to have a good job, nice things and something to call her own. But that wasn't going to happen as long as that proverbial dark cloud continued following her around.

Rayne bit down on her bottom lip, trying to keep the tears at bay. Crying and feeling sorry for herself wasn't going to help. At least that's what she told herself as emotion clogged her throat.

Why me? Why does this stuff always happen to me?

What am I going to do now? played on loop inside her head. So many thoughts ran through her mind at once. How many times would she have to start over? How many times would she pull herself up only to be knocked down again?

"I can't keep going through this."

She shakily climbed out of the car and removed the nozzle from the gasoline pump before realizing she hadn't paid for the gas yet. This was one of those times when a debit or credit card would come in handy instead of cash. She was in no condition to go into the gas station and face anyone, especially knowing that her eyes were probably red and puffy.

I'll do this later. Rayne replaced the nozzle. She needed to pull herself together before she did anything.

"Excuse me," someone called out before Rayne climbed back into the car. A young man, maybe in his early twenties with a white tank top and denim shorts that hung low on his narrow hips, headed toward her. He gave a slight wave.

Despite the friendliness of the man's smile, something felt off. Rayne's heart rate inched up. Anxiety crept through her as he drew closer.

"Sorry to bother you, but can I use your cell phone?" He nodded his head toward a gray sedan parked near the building. "I locked my keys in the car and need to call my brother."

Rayne opened her mouth to respond, but before she spoke, someone hit her from behind. Blinding pain exploded in her skull, and she cried out, reaching to grab onto something, anything as her world started spinning.

Oh, God.

Bile rose to her throat and panic roared through her body as black spots clouded her vision. Her knees went weak. Stumbling, she bumped into a trash can before crumbling to the ground, and the side of her head collided with a concrete slab just before everything went black.

Chapter Sixteen

"You wanted to see me?" Jerry asked from Nick's doorway. He'd been on his way out of the building when the receptionist mentioned that Nick had been looking for him.

His cousin glanced up from his laptop. "Yeah, come in for a minute."

Jerry strolled across the large space and sat in one of the chairs that faced the desk. "What's up?"

"Couple of things. You're all set for the conference in San Antonio. Tammy should've emailed you the hotel and rental car information. I trust that you and CJ can share a vehicle without any problems, right?"

"Yeah, shouldn't be a problem, and I saw emails this morning," Jerry said. He wasn't looking forward to spending five days away from Rayne and Stormy. He already knew if he invited her to go with him, she'd shoot him down, claiming she had to work.

"Also, I'll be meeting with Pilar Tillman to finalize some decisions regarding her new property and the one that she's trying to sell."

"Please tell me that she's ready to make some decisions," Jerry said. They had worked with this customer a few times over the years, and she always had a hard time deciding what she wanted.

"A few, but mainly we need to go over the changes that were made to the plans for her new house," Nick explained. "I know you're trying to finish the Providence property today, but Pilar requested that you be in on this meeting. She wants your opinion on light fixtures for both places."

Jerry studied his cousin, sensing that something else was going on here. "I already gave her a list of the ones that I think would best work in the space."

"Maybe your opinion is not all she wants."

Jerry shook his head and stood. "If you're implying that I've been flirting with her or giving her the impression that I'm giving up more than just my opinion, then you're wrong. Nick, I'm serious about getting that foreman's position. All of my interactions with our customers have been professional. Nothing else."

Nick nodded. "I know. I just wanted to see what you were going to say. I've seen the changes in you. I guess that means that things are getting pretty serious with you and Rayne."

"Yeah. She's it for me," Jerry said simply. "I can't explain how I know or when exactly it happened, but she's the woman I'm going to spend the rest of my life with."

Nick chuckled, running his hand over his low-cut fade. "I get it, man. Been there. That's how it was for me with Sumeera. And my stupid ass almost lost her because I was trying to fight the inevitable."

Jerry smiled, remembering that time. Now Nick and Sumeera were married with a little girl and a baby on the way.

Jerry also thought about something Liam had told him at Nate and Liberty's wedding reception months back.

It's been said that when a Jenkins man meets the one—he immediately knows.

That had definitely been the case for Jerry regarding Rayne. The first few months after she moved in next door, he had thought it crazy that his feelings for her were so strong when he didn't even know her. After a while, all he wanted was to be anywhere she was, even when she shot down his advances.

Jerry leaned on the back of the seat that he had just vacated. "Listen, I'll be here for the meeting, and I'll make it clear to Pilar that the only thing I'm offering her is my knowledge on anything electrical."

Jerry's cell phone vibrated, and he pulled it out of his pocket. When he didn't recognize the number, he let it go to voicemail.

"So, we good?" he asked Nick.

"Yep, but just let Pilar down easy. We ain't tryin' to lose no business here."

Jerry chuckled and headed to the door but stopped when his phone vibrated again. The same telephone number showed on the screen and this time he answered.

"Jerry Jenkins."

"Mr. Jenkins," a professional voice sounded through the phone line, but it was a child crying in the background that caught his attention.

"Yes. Who is this?"

"This is Miss Crawford, the secretary at Starbright Learning Center. I'm calling regarding Stormy."

"Is she all right?"

"Yes, and that's her you're hearing in the background."

"Is she sick? Hurt?"

"Not that we can tell. Her teacher said she was fine earlier, and then all of a sudden she burst into tears. We tried reaching Ms. Ellison, but she hasn't returned our calls. She has you down as an emergency contact."

Rayne had mentioned that to him when she first enrolled Stormy into the summer program, but Jerry never expected to ever get a call.

"Can I get you to at least talk to Stormy? Sometimes just hearing a familiar voice will calm a child."

Worry crept through Jerry. Stormy wasn't a crier. She was good at pouting, but he couldn't ever remember her crying.

"Yes, put her on the phone." He heard some rustling, and the secretary trying to coax Stormy into talking, but she continued crying.

Anxiety grew inside of him, and Jerry rubbed his chest as if that would keep his heart from leaping out.

"I'm sorry, she's still not cooperating. I'll hold the phone to her ear."

"Ladybug? Hey, baby. What's going on?" Jerry called Stormy's name a few more times and she cried harder. Nothing he said helped, which was unusual.

"Is it possible for you to come to the center?" the secretary asked when she got back on the phone.

"I'll be there in ten minutes."

"What happened?" Nick asked after Jerry disconnected the call. "Is Stormy all right?"

Jerry shook his head and dialed Rayne. "No. Somethin's up. I need to go down there since they haven't been able to reach Rayne. Actually, I should've heard from her by now, too. She usually takes a break around this time."

When Jerry got Rayne's voicemail, he left a message, letting her know that the center was trying to reach her and that he was heading there.

"I'm gonna get going, but I'll be back before the meeting."

"Okay, keep me posted. Hopefully, Stormy is all right."

Yeah, hopefully.

Jerry arrived at the center in record time and jogged across the parking lot to the entrance. The moment he was buzzed into the building and started down the hall, he heard Stormy. She wasn't as loud as she'd been a few minutes ago, but it bothered him that she was still upset.

"I want my daddy. I want my daddy!" she cried, catching Jerry off guard. He stopped just before he reached the office, and his heart lodged in his throat. She'd been pretty young when her father died and Jerry had never heard her mention him. Why now?

He strolled up to the office door, where he saw two secretaries at desks that were behind a long counter. One woman was on the phone and the other on the computer. When he glanced to his left, his heart plummeted down to his stomach at the sight of the little girl who had come to mean everything to him. She was sitting in one of the chairs against the wall, her eyes and face puffy from crying.

"Ladybug," he said, and her head jerked toward him.

"Daddy," she sobbed and tore across the room, leaping into his arms.

Daddy?

Stunned into silence, Jerry just held her close and kissed the side of her head. She sniffled, her tiny body shaking against him. Hell, she could call him whatever she wanted. He just didn't like seeing her so upset.

"It's okay. You're okay." He rocked her in his arms.

The woman who was sitting in front of the computer stood. "Mr. Jenkins?"

"Yes, I'm Jerry Jenkins." He moved closer to the desk, and Stormy held him tight. She buried her damp face into the crook of his neck and curled into him, as if afraid he was going to put her down.

Jerry rubbed her back. What the hell had happened? Normally, the moment she saw him, she started talking or planting sloppy kisses against his cheek. She was the happiest kid he knew, and this...this wasn't her.

The school secretary approached the counter, her long red curls bouncing with each step she took. Jerry didn't miss the way her dark gaze did a slow crawl down his body. He was a big guy and used to the reaction, but right now all he wanted were answers.

"I'm Ms. Crawford." Her smile, a bit friendlier than he thought appropriate, brightened and Jerry frowned. I'm the one who called you."

"Did you guys ever find out what happened?"

"As far as anyone knows, nothing happened to Stormy. The teacher tried to get her to tell her what was wrong, but

134

she wouldn't stop crying, saying she wanted her daddy. And we still haven't heard back from Ms. Ellison."

Hearing her mother's name, Stormy sobbed quietly, her arms tightening around Jerry's neck.

"Yeah, I left a message for her mother after I heard from you. I should hear back soon. In the meantime, I'm just going to step out into the hallway for a minute with Stormy and—"

"Actually, I'll need to see some ID before I can let you take her anywhere."

He shifted Stormy in his arms, concerned that she still hadn't said anything, and dug out his wallet. He handed the woman his driver's license."

"*Jerry* Jenkins. Thank you." She returned his license, and he put it away. "If you plan to leave with your daughter, we'll need to get her belongings from the classroom, and she'll need to be signed out."

"All right," he said, not bothering to correct her. "For now, I'm just going to talk to her, but I'll let you know if I decide to take her with me."

Jerry headed out of the office and found a bench a few feet away.

"Okay, Ladybug. You want to tell me what's going on?" Jerry continued rubbing her back. When she still didn't speak, he shifted, forcing her to lift her head. His chest tightened at the sight of her tear stained face.

"Baby, tell me what's wrong. Did someone do something to you?"

She shook her head and wiped at her tears with the back of her hand, but they fell faster. Now he was getting concerned.

"Are you sick? Are you hurt? Talk to me. I can't help if I don't know what's wrong."

"I—I'm sad. I...I want to cry."

"Why are you sad?"

She shrugged her little shoulders and dropped her head to his chest. Instead of asking more questions, he just sat rocking her, hoping that she'd start talking eventually. Minutes ticked by and she remained silent.

"Why did you call me daddy in the office?" he asked quietly, aware of a few people walking through the hallway.

After a long hesitation, Stormy lifted her head slightly. Her teary, light-brown eyes met his.

"I want you to be my daddy and...you make me stop being sad."

Again, she had him at a loss for words. Considering Stormy always had something to tell him, she never mentioned anything about wanting him to be her daddy. Of course, he thought about it a thousand times, but his and Rayne's relationship was still new. Marriage, fatherhood, or anything like that hadn't come up. But Jerry wanted nothing more than to have Rayne as his wife and Stormy as his little girl.

"God, I love you." He kissed her forehead. He wasn't sure if he was crossing a line in telling her that, but he couldn't help himself. It was true. He had fallen in love with her and her mother. "I'm going to always be here for you, and I never want you to be sad. Okay?"

She nodded but didn't say anything.

His cell phone dinged, signaling a text message, and he dug it from his pocket and opened the message.

Martina: **I'm at the Providence house. Where are you?**

Jerry: **Had an emergency at Stormy's school, then heading back to a meeting at J & S. I'll hit you up soon.**

Martina: **Cool. TTYL**

Stormy lifted her head, her droopy eyes red. "Do you have to go?" she asked, her voice hoarse.

"Yeah, I need to get back to work."

Her bottom lip trembled and then the waterworks started over again. "But I do—don't want yo-you to."

He wiped his hands gently over her face. "Baby, you're killing me with these tears. You know your mom and I have to work. Why are you crying?"

"I do-don't know," she sobbed louder, dropping her head back to his chest. He hated seeing her like this. There was no way he could leave her.

"Shhh, stop crying. It's okay." Jerry rocked her and used his free hand to shoot Rayne a quick text that he was taking Stormy with him. He had no idea how she would react, but this was a judgment call. He'd deal with any fallout later.

"All right, Ladybug. Let's go get your things so we can get out of here, okay?"

Jerry expected that news to perk her up since she always wanted to go wherever he went, but all she did was nod and then sighed against his chest.

No cheering.

No smiling.

No, *I'm so excited.*

Nothing. She was just limp in his arms.

And I still haven't heard from Rayne.

Chapter Seventeen

Where the hell is she?

Jerry paced the length of the staff lounge at J & S, trying to figure out where Rayne could be. She still wasn't answering her phone. She hadn't called him back. And he had just found out that she'd been laid off.

Damn. Jerry knew Rayne had to be devastated. Even if she was looking for another job, she had no intention of leaving this one until she found a new one. Seemed she just couldn't catch a break. Now he just hoped she hadn't done anything crazy.

He glanced at the sofa where Stormy had been sleeping for the last couple of hours. Instead of going back to work after they left the center, they went to the house, hoping to find Rayne there. When they checked a few other places that she might've gone, and didn't find her, Jerry had taken Stormy to McDonald's. He had hoped to coax her into eating and playing in the play area. Nothing worked. She wasn't herself. She complained of having a headache, which he assumed was from all of the crying, and shortly after that, she had fallen asleep.

What baffled him though, was that she hadn't asked about Rayne. Even when Jerry told her that they'd hear from her soon, Stormy didn't comment.

"How are you holding up?" Nick asked from the doorway of the staff lounge, his laptop tucked under his arm. "Liam mentioned you being out of control."

After a few hours of not hearing from Rayne, Jerry had been on a rampage. Unfortunately, Liam had been on the receiving end of his anger when he didn't give up Charlee's telephone number fast enough. When Jerry finally reached her and filled her in on what little he knew, she made some calls and found out that Rayne had been laid off.

"I hate waiting," Jerry finally said to Nick. "I hate not knowing where she is. What if she's hurt and somewhere by herself? God, if something happened to her…"

"I know you're worried, but don't go imagining the worse. Her cell phone could be dead, or maybe she just needed a little time to herself. Either way, I'm sure she'll be in touch soon."

Jerry wanted to believe that, but deep down he knew something had happened. Rayne would've called him by now if she could.

"Did you call, Craig?" Nick asked of their cousin-in-law. A former detective, Craig still had connections at the police department. Rayne hadn't been missing long enough to file a missing person's report, but Craig promised to make some calls.

Jerry glanced at his watch. "The meeting still on?"

"Yeah, but I'll give you a pass on this one."

Jerry rubbed the back of his neck, trying to work out some of the stiffness. "Thanks. I was planning to attend, but I can't leave Stormy. I know I could get my mom down here, but even with that, I…"

He stared down at Stormy, her tiny body curled into a ball and her soft snores drifting up to his ears. His heart was so full, it felt as if it would explode.

"I recognize that look," Nick said when Jerry met his gaze. "You can't let her out of your sight. I get it."

Jerry nodded, emotion clogging his throat. He had become so attached to Rayne and Stormy, if anything happened to either of them, he didn't know what he'd do.

Nick squeezed his shoulder. "That's love, man. She's a lucky little girl to have you. Hell, they both are."

Again, Jerry nodded, too choked up to speak. He was the lucky one. All it took was for something like this to happen for him to realize just how important they were in his life.

He hadn't told anyone about Stormy calling him daddy earlier, and she hadn't mentioned it again, but it did have Jerry thinking about his future. Their future.

"I'm not usually a worrier," he said, "but damn if she and her mom don't have my nerves shot."

Nick chuckled and headed to the door. "Well, get used to it. Worrying about their well-being is part of the deal, but having them in your life makes it all worth it."

Jerry jumped when his phone rang. Glancing at the screen, he saw that it was Craig. "Please tell me you know something."

"Found her."

*

Jerry followed a nurse down a long hallway, his nerves as raw as stripped wires as he tried ignoring the usual hospital sounds and smells. He'd only been there a few minutes and already the beeping, doctors and nurses talking to patients, and the crying was starting to get to him. Add the smell of disinfectant and other chemicals and he was about ready to run up out of there—but not without Rayne.

He didn't know how Craig was able to get so much information about what had happened, or how he'd been able to work it to where Jerry could see her, but he would be forever grateful.

Rayne had been at the hospital a few hours. She'd been in and out of consciousness. They hadn't been able to contact anyone on her behalf because she had arrived with no ID. Her cell phone and purse had been stolen along with her car.

Carjacked.

The moment Craig had spoken the words, panic seized Jerry's body. That panic had soon turned to anger when he'd found out about her injuries. Concussion. Bruises. She'd even had to get stitches for a deep cut near her hairline. He wanted to strangle the bastards who had attacked her. The police had apprehended one suspect, but they were still looking for his accomplice.

The nurse Jerry had been walking with slowed when they arrived to an area that had several beds with curtains around them.

"She's in the last bay," the nurse said before excusing herself.

Jerry heard Rayne before he saw her, and his heart slammed against his chest.

"Please, I have to get to my daughter. They're going to take her from me," she cried. "They're going to take her."

"Ma'am, I need you to calm down."

"No! I can't let them take her. I have to get out of here."

Jerry hurried past a couple of occupied beds and stopped when he reached the area where Rayne was laying. The machine she was hooked up to beeped faster as she tried unhooking it from her arm, but the nurse stopped her.

"Rayne," he said, and his breath caught when she faced him. The large rectangular bandage on the side of her forehead stood out like a neon sign, but it was the rest of her that gave him pause.

Her weary, light-brown eyes met his. It was like taking a punch to the gut seeing the unhealthy pallor of her skin. Her long, disheveled hair hung free around her shoulders, and she almost didn't look like herself.

"Jerry," she said on a sob, tear stains streaking her face. "I didn't get Stormy from daycare. The State's going to take her away from me if I don't—"

"Baby, I have her. Stormy is fine. I have her," he repeated when it seemed his words weren't registering. Then she burst into tears.

Jerry gently gathered her in his arms and stared up at the ceiling, silently giving thanks that she was okay. The relief flooding his body almost brought him to his knees, and he had to swallow the emotion clogging his throat.

First Stormy's break down, now Rayne's. He couldn't handle their tears. Seeing them both upset and in pain felt like someone was ripping his heart from his chest.

When the nurse stepped out of the small area, giving them some privacy, Jerry climbed onto the narrow bed to be closer to Rayne. He released an exhausted sigh and a wave of possessiveness seized him. Outside of his immediate family, he had never worried about anyone but himself. Until today. Today he experienced what it was like to almost lose someone he loved.

Rayne put her arm across his waist and snuggled closer. Thank God she was safe.

"I will never let anyone hurt you again."

*

Hours later, Rayne allowed Jerry to guide her up the wide staircase that led to two of his three bedrooms. She hadn't protested when he insisted that she and Stormy stay with him for a few days. In fact, Rayne was grateful for all that he'd done for them. If she didn't know how much he cared about her before, she knew now.

She also appreciated his parents. While at the hospital, Violet and Thomas had stayed in the waiting room with Stormy, who had been sleeping when Rayne was finally released. Even feeling as if she'd been run over by a semi-truck, Rayne couldn't get to her child fast enough. She hadn't wanted to let her go even when Jerry insisted on Stormy riding in her booster seat while he drove them to his place.

When Rayne woke up that morning, she'd been in a great mood knowing that she and Jerry had big plans for the weekend. But she should've known better than to get excited about anything. That's not how her life worked. That morning, all in the span of an hour, her smiles had dissolved into tears and pain. Only someone with her kind of luck could lose their job and get carjacked on the same day.

"Ladybug, we'll get your mommy settled and then I'll fix you something to eat, okay?" Jerry said, interrupting Rayne's thoughts.

"Okay," Stormy said quietly.

Jerry was carrying her in one arm, while his other arm was securely wrapped around Rayne's waist. Rayne was trying not to lean against him too much, but she barely had enough energy to keep her head up. The jackhammer pounding inside her skull was relentless. Her head felt as if it was going to explode.

But it wasn't lost on her that Stormy wasn't her usual talkative self. Jerry had filled Rayne in on her crying spell at the daycare and how despondent her daughter had been since then. Rayne couldn't say much since she herself didn't feel much like talking either. But the bright light that usually shone in her baby's eyes had dimmed and it worried her. Stormy didn't have bad days.

"You and Ladybug can use my bedroom. The sheets are clean and you should be able to find the basics of what you'll need in the bathroom. If—"

"You don't have to give up your room," Rayne insisted, but Jerry shuffled them toward his bedroom as if she hadn't said anything.

"I want you to be comfortable and have plenty of space. I'll use the guest room."

His third bedroom, which was on the ground level, was used as a game room and had a pool table set up in the middle of the space. While the other two bedrooms and two of the bathrooms were on the top level.

Once they stepped into the master bedroom, Jerry set Stormy on her feet and then helped Rayne to the huge, king-size bed. "I know you wanted to shower, but why don't you lay down a little while."

Rayne didn't argue. All she wanted to do was crawl into bed and hold her baby girl until they both fell asleep.

She gently laid her head on the pillow and relief flooded through her body. Her eyes drifted closed but popped open when the bed dipped with Jerry sitting next to her, concern in his eyes. Stormy eased up to him, but Rayne didn't have the energy to coax her daughter into the bed.

"I'm sorry," Rayne said, wanting to tell them both how bad she felt about ruining all of their weekend plans. But the words wouldn't come. Her head throbbed just as much as her heart ached. If only she could turn back time and do that morning over again with different results.

Without a word, Jerry lifted Stormy to his lap and she laid her head against his chest, but her gaze was on Rayne. *What are you thinking, baby?* Rayne wanted to ask her child but didn't have the energy. And for the first time since she'd been able to talk in complete sentences, Stormy didn't tell her what was on her mind.

Jerry ran his hand gently over Rayne's hair, and a calmness washed over her. She tried to fight the sleepiness that was slowly pulling her under, but it was too strong. She could barely keep her eyes open.

"Get some sleep." Jerry leaned over and kissed Rayne's cheek. "Me and Ladybug will be back to wake you up in an hour."

Before Rayne could respond, sleep overpowered her.

Chapter Eighteen

"CJ, I don't know what to do," Jerry said into the cell phone that was plastered against his ear as he paced the length of the family room. His sister had called to coordinate plans for their business trip to San Antonio that was coming up in a couple of weeks, but his focus these days was off.

"Do about what?"

"I don't know what to do about Rayne. It's been three days, and she's still not herself. I'm not sure how to help her." Jerry knew he sounded like a wuss, but he wanted his girls back to normal. Even his little chatterbox, Stormy, still wasn't herself.

"I'm sure you being there for Rayne is helping. But, Jay, you gotta realize that's she's been through a traumatic experience. It's demeritorious that she lost her job and got carjacked within minutes of each other. But even more vexatious, she had to be terrified when those guys took her car."

Jerry rolled his eyes at his sister's overuse of words that most people didn't know the meaning of. Off and on over the years, she went on a *learn a new word a day* spree, and the family had to put up with her using them during every conversation. Normally, he would tell her to speak English, but she was right about Rayne.

"I think the ordeal is still freaking her out. She's been jumpier than usual, and though she's been sleeping a lot, I don't think it's been a good sleep."

"Can you blame her? Every time she closes her eyes, she's probably reliving that day. Give her some time to recover. She's been through hell mentally and physically. It's scary just thinking about getting mugged, let alone having your car stolen."

Jerry knew his sister was right. The police had finally caught the second guy involved, and thankfully they both had warrants out for their arrest. According to Craig, they could get two to eight years of jail time and a hefty fine.

As far as Jerry was concerned, that wasn't punishment enough. Rayne was left with injuries, as well as fear, and for that Jerry wanted to beat their asses.

"I'm thinking about taking Rayne and Stormy with me when we go to San Antonio. They can hang out at the hotel while we attend workshops."

"That's a good idea. Luke was planning to come with me, but they're working on a big case and he doesn't think he can get away."

Christina's husband had been a defense attorney in New York before moving to Cincinnati. Now he was an attorney at Jerry's uncle's law firm.

"Do you think Rayne will agree to go?"

Jerry rubbed the back of his neck. Rayne was barely speaking to him or anyone for that matter. Even Charlee couldn't get through to her after flying back to town the day after the incident. She had spent the day with Rayne while Jerry was at work, and later confided in him that she'd never seen Rayne so despondent.

"Jerry?" Christina called out.

"Yeah, I'm here, and to answer your question, I don't know if Rayne will agree to go, but I can't leave them here. I need them with me."

"Aww, look at you. My little brother is finally growing up and thinking about someone other than himself," CJ cracked.

Jerry didn't respond because it was true. As the baby in the family, he'd admit that he was spoiled, and rarely did he think of anyone other than himself.

But Rayne and Stormy had quickly found their way into his heart. They were a part of his life, and their happiness and safety were his top priority. They'd been through enough, especially Rayne, and he wanted to be the one to give them a different type of life. But he was so out of his element, Jerry feared one wrong move on his part might have Rayne putting her guards back up, or worse, leaving him.

"Listen, I know you're worried about Rayne, but I think in this situation, you're going to have to give her time to recover. All you can do is be there for her, and it can't hurt to *ask* if she wants to go to San Antonio with you. Just be prepared if she says no."

No wasn't an option. He wasn't leaving them in Cincinnati alone, and he couldn't miss this conference. Nick had pretty much promised him the foreman's job, and Jerry wanted to show his cousin that he wouldn't let personal problems stop him from doing his job.

His other concern about asking Rayne to go to San Antonio was her past. Would she even consider going back to the town that held so many bad memories?

"You know what?" Christina said.

"What?"

"If you're that concerned about your woman, get mom to talk to her. If anyone can get her back on her feet, it's Violet Jenkins."

Jerry nodded in agreement even though Christina couldn't see him. A few minutes later, he took her advice and called their mother.

"Hey, sweetheart," she answered on the first ring, her voice as cheerful as usual.

"Hey, Mom. I...I need your help."

*

Rayne slowly opened her eyes. For the first time in days, her brain didn't feel as if it was trying to claw its way out of her head. The bruise on the back of her head and cut on the side of her forehead were still tender, but at least the aches were bearable.

A light knock sounded at the bedroom door before it swung open. Rayne expected Stormy to walk in, but instead, Violet floated in carrying a tray of food.

It always amazed Rayne how the older woman moved with such grace, like she was floating on a cloud, her feet barely touching the floor.

"Oh good, you're awake. Good morning."

"Morning."

Rayne eased up in bed, pulling the sheet up to her waist. She hadn't expected anyone other than Jerry and Stormy, and was glad she wore nice lounging pajamas. When Charlee had flown in for a day, she had packed up some of Rayne and Stormy's clothes and brought them to Jerry's place.

Violet set the tray at the foot of the bed then glided to the windows, her long floral dress billowing around her ankles. With the theatrics of an actress, she gripped the curtains and swung her arms out, opening them with a dramatic flourish.

"It's such a beautiful day," she said wistfully, as if seeing the sun for the first time ever.

Rayne watched with interest as the woman held her head back, closed her eyes, then smiled as she stood soaking up the rays.

Clearly, she loved life's simple pleasures. If Rayne had just a little of Violet's vivaciousness, she could dig out of the rut she seemed to keep falling into.

When I grow up, I want to be just like her.

The random thought almost brought a smile to Rayne's face. Instead, she squinted against the burst of sunlight that poured into the room.

Violet adjusted the curtains, then moved back to the bed.

"I heard you haven't been eating, and I think it's time we changed that. How do you feel?"

"Better." At least physically, Rayne thought. Mentally and emotionally, she couldn't seem to pull herself together. "How are you?" she asked, accepting the tray of food Violet handed her.

"I'm well, but I'm concerned about you and thought it was time I stopped by for a visit."

Rayne gave a slight nod, but she really wasn't up for company. Instead of saying that though, her gaze dropped to the food on the tray.

"My little helper downstairs would be very disappointed if you didn't eat what she has prepared. She told me that grilled cheese sandwiches and apples with peanut butter are your favorites. Stormy also mentioned that you like gummy bears with your lunch," Violet said seriously, with a twinkle in her eyes.

Rayne smiled. Her heart melted as she looked at the tray filled with her daughter's favorite foods.

"God, I love that kid," she said more to herself than Violet. Rayne realized how much she missed hugging and talking to her baby girl.

"And she loves you." Violet grabbed one of the cups of tea that was on the tray and sat in the upholstered chair that Jerry had moved close to the bed days ago. "She also misses you. We all do."

Rayne's stomach tightened at that last comment. She missed them too. Even having Jerry, and Stormy around daily, Rayne felt as lost and lonely as she had when Kirk died. She couldn't shake the heavy weight pressing down on her chest.

"Oh, and the Tylenol is from Jerry." Violet gestured to the unopened medicine bottle sitting on the tray next to the apple juice. "He said you'd probably need it."

Guilt lodged in Rayne's throat. Jerry had been by her side and had taken care of Stormy as if they were his responsibility. He hadn't asked anything of Rayne. He wasn't stressing her to snap out of whatever funk she was in. And he hadn't complained while she wallowed in self-pity.

No one had ever taken care of her the way he'd been doing.

"Maybe we can chat while you *eat*." Violet sipped her tea, steam rising above the rim.

Even though she wasn't really hungry, Rayne felt obligated to at least taste the food. She started with the grilled cheese sandwich that had been cut diagonally...just the way she always cut Stormy's.

Rayne bit into the sandwich and tears filled her eyes, but no way was she going to cry in front of Violet.

God, what is wrong with me?

"I don't know what my problem is," Rayne choked out, resting her head against the headboard. "I miss Jerry and Stormy so much. Even though they've been by my side every day, I can't seem to shake this...this..." Rayne sighed, frustrated that she couldn't find the words to express what exactly she was feeling.

"I won't pretend to know what you're going through, but I recognize depression when I see it." Violet set her mug on the nightstand. Leaning forward in her seat, she reached for Rayne's hand. "Sweetheart, I know the last few days have been rough, and it takes time to bounce back. But you can't stop living when bad things happen."

"I feel like a failure. All of my life I've tried to turn bad situations into good ones. Yet, each time I think that I'm finally on the right track and have taken the right path, I get sideswiped and knocked on my butt. I'm so tired of trying."

"What would be the alternative?"

Giving up, Rayne wanted to say but wouldn't dare speak the words out loud. She might get down on herself and have considered giving up more times than she could count, but she never did. *And I never will.*

The words floated inside her mind, but right now she was having a hard time believing them.

"I don't have a job. I don't have a car. I don't have money, and without those things, I'm not going to have a place to live. I—"

"Stop talking about what you don't have and look at what you do have. You have the sweetest little girl downstairs who misses her mommy. You have a wonderful man who is crazy about you despite what you have or don't have. You have brains, beauty, and a resiliency that many people don't possess.

"Don't let your circumstances control you, Rayne. You're better than that. You're stronger than that," Violet said with conviction, still holding onto Rayne's hand. "And on top of that, you have us. You have *a family* who will help you any way we can."

A family. Rayne started shaking her head but stopped when she was immediately reminded that it still hurt. She was too afraid to believe...or hope for a family like theirs. She had avoided getting close to people for years, afraid that they'd abandon her the way others had. It didn't matter that she loved Jerry, their relationship was too new for his mother to consider Rayne family.

"If my relationship with Jerry fails, you won't—"

"What makes you think it will fail?"

"Because I have nothing to offer him," Rayne snapped before catching herself. "Your son is an amazing man...the total package. There are women out there ready to fall at his feet. I have seen the way they look at him. Jerry can have anyone he wants, bu—"

"But he chose you." Violet released Rayne's hand and sat back in her seat. "I've never had low self-esteem. So forgive my lack of tact for what I'm about to say. If you don't think you're worthy of Jerry, you're probably not. And you're going to lose him."

Ouch.

"You're going to eventually push him away with negativity and self-doubt that you probably don't even realize you're portraying."

Rayne didn't respond, but Violet was right. Jerry hated when she talked down on herself in any manner, and her negativity would probably get old real soon. She had to pull herself together before she lost the best thing that ever happened to her.

"And regarding those other women who are ready to fall at his feet, make sure they know that he's not available. Sweetheart, the Jenkins men are like babe magnets."

Rayne laughed.

"I'm serious. You should've seen the women I had to deal with when I was dating Thomas. Heck, even now, I still have to give some of them the evil eye for checking him out. If you witness it with *your man*, don't just accept that disrespect. Say something or do something."

Violet crossed one leg over the other, swinging her foot back and forth. "What does Jerry do when women give him too much attention?" his mother asked.

Rayne thought back on a couple of instances months ago. She hadn't said anything to him back then because they were just friends. Now that they were dating, she saw the attention he garnered, but because he never did or said anything to encourage other women, Rayne hadn't said anything to him or the women. And that's what she told Violet.

Eating a little more of her lunch, Rayne wondered if that's where she went wrong with Kirk. Women were attracted to him, touching his arm while smiling in his face, but Rayne had ignored the few incidents that she'd witnessed. She thought that being married to him was enough to keep other women away. Boy had she been wrong.

"Jerry is committed to you, Rayne. If he does something inappropriate, call him out on it, and make sure he knows that you're not accepting that type of behavior. And If a woman makes a play for him, snatch her up and tell her to back the hell off. He's yours."

Rayne nodded, hoping to never get into that situation, but Jerry was a man that she'd fight for.

Violet stood. "Oh, and as far as you having a family, I have adopted you and Stormy into our family. No matter what happens between you and my son, I'll always be here for you two."

Rayne put her hand on her chest and tried to swallow the emotion settling in her throat. Having a family was all she ever really wanted.

"Thank you," she finally choked out.

"Are you done eating?"

"Yes, I'm done."

Now that she had eaten some and her mind was a little clearer, Rayne felt better than she'd felt in days. It would be a while before she forgot about the carjacking, but at least she didn't feel as hopeless about her current situation.

"Thanks, Violet, for everything. I appreciate the meal and the talk."

Violet hugged her. "It's my pleasure, sweetheart. Remember what I said about not letting your circumstances control you. I hate what you've been through, but you're a survivor. You're going to get through this trial and be better because of it."

Rayne nodded. "I believe I will. Thanks again."

"Anytime."

After Violet left the room, Rayne eased out of bed and went to the bathroom to freshen up. While she was in there, she thought about all that she and Violet had discussed. Rayne had been so young when her mother gave her up, and she never had anyone to talk to her as candidly as Violet had. She had known shortly after meeting Jerry's mother that she would like her, and Rayne looked forward to building on their relationship.

She strolled back into the bedroom, but instead of climbing into the bed, she moved to the window. She imitated what Violet had done earlier, closing her eyes and soaking up the heat from the sun.

A slow smile spread across her mouth. She had to admit, the sunlight did feel good on her skin.

"Mommy!" Stormy called out before plowing into the room, excited energy bouncing off of her.

153

That sparkle that had been missing from her eyes for the last few days had returned, and Rayne's spirits lifted even higher. Her baby was back to her usual self.

"Guess what?" she said, bouncing up and down.

"What?"

"Jerry said I've been a big girl. Now I can get a puppy!" she screeched, sending chill bumps down Rayne's arms. She didn't get a chance to respond because Jerry showed up in the doorway.

Rayne's breath caught. He'd had a meeting earlier and apparently hadn't had a chance to change clothes. He looked so good in a light-blue, button-down dress shirt, and dark slacks that made his long legs seem even longer.

"For the record. I did not say Stormy was getting a puppy."

"But…but, I'm a big girl now."

Rayne laughed and kissed her daughter. When she glanced up, Jerry was strolling into the room. His eyes zoned in on her like a heat-seeking vessel and her pulse kicked up. The sexual magnetism that made him so irresistible was in full effect and all Rayne wanted to do was fall into his arms and hold on tight.

Yep. Definitely a babe magnet.

Chapter Nineteen

"Hey, beautiful. You are definitely a sight for sore eyes," Jerry said and carefully gathered Rayne into his arms, not wanting to jostle her too much. He held her a few minutes, soaking up her essence then bent down and covered her mouth with his.

While she'd been recovering, he kissed her daily, but this was the first time in days that she hungrily kissed him back.

"Ewww," Stormy squealed.

Jerry chuckled against Rayne's lips, and when they looked over, Stormy had her hands over her eyes grinning. They tried to keep their kisses rated G whenever she was around, but today Jerry couldn't help himself.

He glanced back at Rayne. "It's good to see you up and moving around. How do you feel?"

She cupped his cheek and smiled. It had been too many days since those gorgeous light-brown eyes stared up at him with such passion. He had even been afraid that he would never see her smile again.

"I feel better than I've felt in a while. Thanks for putting up with me."

"Always."

"Stormy," Violet called from downstairs. "Come here, Sweetie."

"Here I come." Stormy tore out of the room.

"Ladybug, no running down the stairs," Jerry called after her.

"Okay," she said, her distant voice sounding as if she was already halfway down the stairs.

Rayne slid her hand into his. "Thanks for sicking your mom on me."

"I have no idea what you're talking about." Jerry feigned innocence, but then winked.

With her hand in his, he moved across the room and sat in the chair he had put next to the bed. He guided Rayne to sit on his lap, glad she didn't protest. He just wanted to hold her, if only for a few minutes.

"You sure you're doing okay?" he asked, searching her eyes as if that would give him the answers he needed. His heart was finally beating normally. The past few days had been hard on all of them, but especially Rayne. She still looked a little pale, but she was moving around better.

"My head still hurts some, but I'm doing okay." She fingered one of the buttons on his shirt. "I owe you an apology. I'm sorry for shutting down on you. I can't promise it won't happen again, but I'm going to get myself together to ensure that it doesn't. Thank you for being here for me and my baby."

"Sweetheart, I love you. I never knew I was capable of loving someone as much as *I love you*. There is no other place I want to be than with you and Stormy."

He didn't miss the surprise in her eyes. That had been the first time he had actually professed those words to her.

"I told you before, I'm here for the long haul. I understand why you shut down. I totally get it. I was just afraid that you'd get too deep inside your head and not be able to find your way back to me."

Rayne wrapped both arms around him. "I love you, too. I love you so much it scares me," she said, her voice muffled against his neck.

They sat like that, holding each other for the longest. Jerry never wanted to let her go, but they still had a few issues to work out.

"Listen," he said, and she leaned back, searching his eyes. He didn't know what she saw, but he needed to erase the worry from her face. "Relax. It's nothing bad. I have something for you."

He reached over to the nightstand and opened the top drawer, pulling out a box. When he handed it to Rayne, her eyes grew large.

"You bought me a cell phone?" she asked. "Jerry, this is too much. I can't acce—"

"Yes, you can and you will. You need a phone, and they had a special going. Since I was due for an upgrade, I was able to get a good deal on a second device."

"I'm going to pay you back."

He knew she would say something like that. It was okay to be independent, but sometimes she drove him nuts not wanting him to do anything for her.

"You're not paying me back. That's a gift. Besides, you were due for a new one, and I need to be able to reach you. Now, let's talk about your car."

He had already told her that the cops had found it, along with her purse and driver's license. She'd only had a few dollars in her wallet, which the punks took, but thankfully she hadn't had any credit cards.

"I know you said that you don't want the car back."

"I don't. I'm not sure I'll ever want to drive again, but I can't see that car without thinking about..."

"Okay," Jerry said, rubbing her back, not wanting her to think about that day. "At some point, you're going to want and need a car, and I might've found you one. My aunt is selling her Ford Edge and it'll be perfect for you."

"Jerry...I can't afford—"

"Stop." He gave her a quick kiss on the forehead to quiet her. "Don't get all worked up. We'll figure out all of that. The good news is that I already know someone who will buy your old car. So that money can go toward another vehicle."

"Okay."

"Now, we need some ground rules. For now on, we need to do a better job in keeping in contact throughout the day. Even a short text will work. When I couldn't find you the other day, I was worried half to death.

"Also, when something bad happens, like the layoff, call me, or my mom, or somebody, especially if you're on edge. In the past, you've had to deal with everything on your own. Those days are gone. You have people who love you and care about your well-being. Don't shut us out.

"Lastly, for now on, I'll be putting the gas in your car."

She sighed. "Jerry. That's not necessary. At some point, I'll be okay and able to visit a gas station again."

"That's not the only reason I'll be doing it." He pushed hair out of her face. "I want to take care of you, Rayne. All of my life, I've watched my father take care of my mother, doing everything like filling her gas tank, keeping her car clean, and going shopping with her, to name a few. I've always admired the way he treats her, and I planned to make sure you and Stormy are treated the same way, if you'll let me."

After a long hesitation, she said, "I'd like that, but Jerry, you have to understand. I've never been around couples who were in loving relationships. Until I met your parents, I haven't had any example of what that looks like, and I've never had a real family. Because of that, I'm afraid I'm going to screw up our relationship."

"You're not going to screw up anything. I'll admit, growing up as a Jenkins, I have had plenty of positive examples of what love looks like. That doesn't mean that *I'm* not going to screw up. But I plan to treat you the way I want to be treated, and the way I'd want the women in my life to be treated."

"But what if I don't or can't give you what you need or expect?"

"Do you know why I fell for you?"

"No."

"Not only are you fine as hell with a slammin' body, but I like the way I feel when I'm with you," he said, the worry on her face softening. "You make me want to be a better man. You make me want to be there whenever you and Stormy need me. I like who I am when I'm with you."

"God, I love you," she said.

"And that's all I need."

She looked more tired than she had when he first walked into the room.

"I think you should get back in bed, but there's one more thing we need to discuss."

"What's that?"

"I want you and Stormy to go to San Antonio with me."

Chapter Twenty

"Have I mentioned that I'm a little anxious about flying. I hope I don't freak out on the airplane and embarrass you."

Jerry chuckled. He reached across the console of his truck and squeezed Rayne's hand. "You're going to be fine."

They were on their way to pick up Stormy from his parents' house, and from there they were heading to the airport. For the first time since Nick asked him to attend the conference, Jerry was looking forward to the trip.

"I'm just glad you agreed to go with me."

"You didn't give me much choice with those persuasive kisses and promises of rest, relaxation, and a big surprise. Which I plan to hold you to. Oh, and let's not forget the guilt-tripping," she cracked.

"I did not guilt you into going with me."

"Really? You're going to sit over there and tell that lie?"

"Okay, maybe I exaggerated the part about Nick firing me, but—"

"Yeah, that's what I thought. But seriously, I am looking forward to the trip. And Stormy is so excited, she could barely get to sleep last night. I think a little vacation is just what we both need."

During one of their conversations, Rayne had casually mentioned that she had never spent more than a night in a hotel, and that had been her wedding night. Nor had she ever been on a real vacation.

So many of their conversations ended with Jerry realizing how blessed he'd been to have a great childhood. Even as an adult, his life's challenges were nothing compared to what she'd had to endure. And though a big part of this trip was business, he planned to make sure she and Stormy had a good time.

"I'm glad you're feeling better," he said, splitting his attention between her and the road.

Rayne smiled at him, something she'd been doing more of over the last couple of weeks. "Yeah, me too."

It was good to have her almost back to normal. The headaches weren't as frequent, and she wasn't as jumpy as she'd been after the carjacking. She had even moved her and Stormy back home, even though he wanted them to stay with him awhile longer, but Jerry understood. Moving back to her house had restored some of her sense of independence.

Now all they had to do was find her a job. To take some of her worries away, he had planned to cover her rent short term, but his parents had beat him to it. They gifted her money to cover two month's rent.

At first, Rayne balked at the offer, but she was no match for Violet's determination when it came to doing something she wanted to do. Jerry was glad to see that things were slowly starting to look up for Rayne. She even had an interview scheduled with his uncle's law firm once she returned from San Antonio. It wasn't a guaranteed job, but it was something.

*

"Mommy! Jerry!" Were the first words Rayne heard when Jerry let them into his parent's home. They were standing in the foyer as Stormy ran down the hall towards them pulling a pink, rolling suitcase, and Violet followed behind her.

"Look." Stormy beamed, showing them the front of the Princess Tiana suitcase. "My Nana bought me this."

"Nana?" Rayne and Jerry said in unison.

Violet shrugged. "What? Rayne won't let her call me Violet. I had to come up with something other than Mrs. Jenkins."

Jerry shook his head, and Rayne smiled. She fell more in love with his mother every day.

"And Mr. Jenkins new name is Papa." Stormy bounced up and down on her toes, grinning. "And when I come back, my Papa is getting me a swing in his back yard. And my suitcase has new clothes."

Jerry shook his head. "Mom, Rayne already packed for Stormy. Why would you buy her more stuff? Our suitcases are already in the truck and there's not enough room for—"

"First of all, I can spend my money anyway I want. Secondly, go get her suitcase out of the truck. You guys can just add some of these items to what's already packed. Problem solved." When Jerry didn't make a move to go back outside, Violet pointed at the door. "Go get it."

He huffed out a breath. "Fine."

Rayne smiled and hugged Violet. "Thank you for all that you do for us," she whispered in her ear.

"I love doing for you girls," she whispered back, holding Rayne tight. "Be sure to have a good time this week, and only positive thoughts while you're away, okay?"

Rayne nodded. "Okay."

If Rayne would've had a choice of mothers when she was growing up, she would've wanted one just like Violet. The woman was everything she hoped to be one day. Self-assured, full of life, and one of the kindest people Rayne had ever met. Violet was turning into the mother she never had but always wanted, and Rayne had never felt so loved.

So this is what it's like to have a family.

Twenty minutes later, they had transferred everything Stormy needed to the new suitcase, and Violet had packed a few snacks for them to take on the plane.

"All right, Mom, we'd better get going," Jerry said before kissing Violet on the cheek. "We don't want to miss our flight."

Violet hugged Rayne and Stormy. "Well, you guys have a good, safe trip. Text and let us know you got there okay."

"Will do." Jerry grabbed a hold of Rayne's hand and headed to the front door.

Rayne always felt special by the gesture. From the moment she agreed to be his woman, Jerry started holding her hand wherever they went. His parents were hand-holders, and his father had once told him that he and Violet held hands to show their solidarity. To show the world that they were an impenetrable pair. They never let people walk between them, sit between them, or come between them. Not even their children.

Rayne thought that was so romantic, and she loved that Jerry wanted to start that same tradition with her.

My life is finally looking up.

Now all she had to do was get over her fear of flying. She still couldn't believe that she let Jerry talk her into going back to San Antonio. But when he said that he wouldn't go since he couldn't leave her and Stormy behind, Rayne conceded.

Yep, my life is definitely looking up.

Chapter Twenty-One

Hours later, Rayne dragged into their one-bedroom suite, exhausted from the long day. But she perked up when she noticed the wall of windows and the view. Before she could say anything or make her way across the room, Stormy ran past her.

"Ooh, we're all the way up to the sky. I can see a lot. Come look, Mommy."

Rayne's gaze traveled over the impressive suite, taking in the earth tones and modern decor as she walked to the windows.

"Wow, you're right, kiddo. We are pretty high up and we're overlooking the River Walk."

"The River Walk? We can walk on it?" Stormy asked, her forehead pressed against the window pane.

"We can walk on the sidewalk that goes around the river," Rayne explained. Her child took words so literally, the last thing Rayne wanted was for her to try walking on the river.

"One day this week, we'll take a boat tour around the River Walk," Jerry said, absently.

Through the window, Rayne could see him behind them, roaming around the space, thoroughly checking out the room. She turned around, watching as he inspected the small kitchenette area, then went into the bedroom before returning to the main area.

"I guess this is going to have to do," he finally said. "I had hoped that by the time we arrived, that one of the two-bedroom suites would've been available. Unfortunately, the hotel is totally booked."

Rayne approached the bedroom, liking the double-door entrance. Inside, the room was huge with a king size bed, dresser with a television on top of it, and an upholstered chair and a small table near the window. The bed looked so comfortable that she was tempted to climb into it right then. Their flight out of Cincinnati had been delayed by three hours and now it was almost nine o'clock in the evening, but felt more like midnight.

She ambled into the attached bathroom that was all white and chrome with a long vanity. "This is cool. There are two entrances into the bathroom," she said.

"Let me see," Stormy said when she walked in, Jerry right behind her.

"You and Ladybug take the bedroom, and I'll use the pull-out couch," Jerry said from the bathroom doorway that led to the living room.

"This is pretty," Stormy said, touching the items on top of the vanity. "I'm gonna go look at the river thing again." She ran off, leaving the room just as fast as she had entered.

"I don't like the idea of you having to sleep on the sofa," Rayne said to Jerry, but couldn't think of any other alternative. She would love nothing better than to share that huge, king size bed with him, but that wasn't going to happen with Stormy being with them.

"I've slept on worse," he said, but eyed her sheepishly, probably remembering how she'd been homeless. "I guess we all have, huh?"

"Yeah." Rayne walked up to him, and he wrapped his arms around her.

She wasn't going to think about being homeless or anything else that wasn't positive. Driving from the airport to the hotel had already been like traveling down a memory lane with potholes. Thankfully, they hadn't gone through either of her old neighborhoods. That would've been too hard to handle, and no way she could've stayed positive.

Jerry held her close to his body and Rayne soaked up his warmth. She inhaled deeply. The woodsy scent of his cologne surrounded her, creating a feeling of home in his embrace.

"God, I love you," he said into her hair, placing a kiss above her temple, near the area where she'd had stitches. Since having them removed the day before, Jerry had been planting kisses near that spot. Rayne wasn't sure if it was intentional or if he was doing it subconsciously. Either way, she liked the contact.

"I love you, too."

It had been a little over two weeks since the carjacking, and except for the occasional headache, she had recovered from her injuries. Still a little jumpy around people, Rayne was slowly getting back to herself. Jerry, on the other hand, was still hovering, insisting on taking her everywhere she needed to go. The last couple of days he had lightened up, but only because he'd been super busy at work.

"You doing okay?" he asked, for what seemed like the hundredth time that day.

"Yes, I'm good. What about you?"

"With you in my arms, I'm great. Did I mention that I'm glad you agreed to come with me?"

She leaned back and smiled. "You might've mentioned it a couple of times." She wanted to tell him that she'd go anywhere with him, but kept that thought to herself.

"You look a little tired."

"Is that your way of trying to get me into bed?"

His infamous grin that peeked out on occasion made an appearance. "Is it working?"

Rayne laughed. "Yeah, but considering how much I want you, it wouldn't take much to talk me into bed," she whispered, her hands sliding down his chest, over his torso, and then she gripped his butt, pulling him against the front of her body.

"Girl, don't be playin'." He nuzzled her neck, his hands on her hips as he moved against her. "I've been walking around with a semi-hard-on for weeks. It's only a matter of time before I explode. *Soon*. Soon you will be mine in every way."

Rayne moaned, wondering when *soon* would present itself. Weeks ago, the carjacking had ruined their romantic weekend plans. Since then, Jerry had been handling her like fine china that he was afraid he would break. Thanks to Violet, they'd had some alone time, but even when Rayne made a pass at him, he'd have her to slow her roll, claiming that she was still recovering.

"Mommy. Jerry," Stormy called from the other room, giving Rayne and Jerry time to pull apart. "I'm hungry."

"Yeah, me too, Ladybug. I'll go get us something while you guys get settled. Any special requests?" He looked at Rayne, lust radiating in his eyes.

"Yeah, I have a few, but I'll tell you later." She winked and walked out of the bathroom thinking that *soon* better get there quick.

*

"The end," Stormy said and closed the book.

While Jerry was out getting them dinner, she and Rayne sat in the bed first looking through magazines and now it was story time.

Violet, bless her heart, had signed Stormy up for a children's book subscription, and they had received the first three books the other day. Rayne couldn't think of a better gift for her child.

"Do you want to read this time?" Stormy asked, pulling another book from her bag.

"I love listening to you. How about you read another one?" Rayne still wasn't able to read more than a few pages without getting a headache.

"Okay, I'll read one more, but that's it."

Rayne smiled and shook her head. Her little girl was growing up too fast.

Soon she'll be going off to college.

That thought made her heart ache as she recalled the conversation with Jerry. Who was she kidding? She wanted a family, a larger family, but was scared to death to even wish for something like that. Sure, she and Stormy had been adopted by the Jenkins', but that wasn't a substitute for what Rayne really wanted—her own family. She wanted a husband and more children.

Stormy glanced over her shoulder. "Mommy, are you listening?"

Rayne bit back a laugh. "Yes, I'm listening, but can you sit a little closer to me? I want to hold you."

"Sure."

She scooted back and Rayne put her arms around her daughter and kissed the top of her head before she ran her fingers through the long strands.

Stormy opened the next book, sifted through a couple of pages, but didn't start reading. "Mommy?"

"Yes, sweetheart."

"I told Jerry I want him to be my daddy." Rayne stiffened, and her hand stilled in Stormy's hair as she sat stunned by her daughter's admission.

"Wh—when did you tell him that?"

"A long time ago when you fell and you hurt your head. I was at school. Remember when I was crying?"

"I remember. You were sad, and I was sad, too. What did Jerry say when you asked him to be your daddy?" And Rayne wondered why he never mentioned this conversation.

"He said he loved me. He never want me to be sad again." She put the book down and turned fully to Rayne. "Can you get married so Jerry can be my daddy? Please."

Again, Stormy left her speechless and all Rayne could do was stare at her child. Every day they both fell more in love with Jerry, and he had shown them on so many occasions how much he loved them. But marriage...

"I'm not sure, sweetheart. I'll have to talk to Jerry about that." *One day*, she thought, hoping her response would be enough for now.

There were times when Rayne feared that things were moving too fast between her and Jerry, but whenever she looked up and saw love shining in his eyes, her...

The hotel room door slammed. "Where my girls at?" Jerry called out.

Stormy scurried off the bed just as he made an appearance in the doorway of the bedroom. His hands were full with a large pizza box and several plastic bags, but his gaze was solely on Rayne. And then he frowned.

"What's wrong? You feel okay?"

Rayne's heart flipped in her chest and she swallowed hard. *That's the look.* That was the look she often saw in his eyes that turned her worries into believing that they would have a future together. That their love for each other was stronger than anything she had ever experienced.

"Rayne?" He walked toward her.

"I feel fine," she said quickly. "As a matter of fact, I feel better than I have in years."

And it's all because of you.

Chapter Twenty-Two

"Okay, stop right here," Jerry said to Rayne as they stood outside of their hotel suite. With the help of Christina, he had been able to set his surprise for Rayne into motion. Not only had his sister entertained Stormy and Rayne earlier, but she had also agreed to let his ladybug stay the night with her.

"Close your eyes," Jerry said to Rayne. He pulled a scarf out of his front pocket and tied it around her eyes.

"Really, Jerry?" Rayne giggled. She'd been giddy since they left the bar in anticipation of his surprise. "I don't need the blindfold. My eyes are closed."

"I'm not taking any chances. You might decide to peek before I'm ready to show you your surprise."

He unlocked the door and carefully guided her inside the room where they were greeted by soft jazz that he had left playing.

"Okay, stop right here and don't move."

"Mmm, something smells good. I'm suddenly a little hungry."

Yeah, Jerry was hungry too, but not for food. His woman looked hella good in the low-cut, short black dress that hugged her luscious curves, and he couldn't wait to get her out of it. But tonight, he wanted to wine and dine Rayne, make her feel like the special woman she was. Not like just one of his other conquests.

He went to the small dining table that held their meal and lit the candle before moving on to the other candles that were set up around the suite.

"Can I just say, you look sexy as hell in that dress?"

Rayne smiled demurely. "Thank you." She nervously touched the blindfold before her hands roamed blindly over her full hips.

All night she'd been self-conscious about the short dress. Earlier, when they were hanging out in the hotel's bar, she kept fidgeting with the top of the garment, probably not realizing that she was bringing more attention to her full breasts with every move she made. Then there were the moments where she squirmed on the bar stool, tugging on the hem of the dress attempting to cover up her gorgeous, shapely legs.

Jerry gave the room a quick once over before moving back to where she was standing.

"Okay, I'm going to take off your blindfold."

When he removed the covering from Rayne's eyes, she released a wistful sigh, and her hand went to her chest.

"Oh, Jerry. Everything looks so beautiful."

She moved through the dimly lit, main living area of the suite and followed the pink and red rose petals that started at the door. She stopped at the crystal vase of red roses that were on top of the sofa table and inhaled.

Taking time to smell the roses.

Jerry watched with interest. He already knew she appreciated some of the most simplest gestures. Her humbleness and past experiences made him want to give her the world, show her a different side of humanity.

"Soft jazz, rose petals, dinner...I didn't know you were a romantic."

"Only with you, baby."

He reached for Rayne's hand and brought it to his lips, placing a kiss on the inside of her wrist. He guided her across the room to the table that was set for two. There had never been another woman that he wanted to impress, a woman he wanted to express his love to. He hadn't been kidding when he told her that she made him want to be a better man, a better person. For so many years he only had to be responsible for himself. It was nice putting someone else's needs ahead of his own for a change.

Jerry pulled out the chair at the table for her, and immediately his attention was drawn to the back of her dress. The clingy garment hugged her perfectly round ass and brought attention to her enticing full hips.

He loved her full-figured body and couldn't wait to see all of her. The outfit was doing wicked things to his body, and if he didn't get his libido under control, he was going to move faster than intended and ruin the evening.

Once she was seated, Jerry removed the stainless-steel food covers, revealing honey-hoisin glazed pork tenderloin, roasted potatoes with peppers, and a side salad.

"That looks delicious."

"I'm glad you think so. When we're done with dinner, there are chocolate covered strawberries for dessert." He poured them both a glass of champagne and handed one to Rayne. "Here's to us and many more romantic evenings."

They clinked glasses, took a sip, and dived into their meal. As they ate and talked, the illumination from the candles, that were placed strategically around the room, cast just enough light on Rayne's gorgeous face. She really was a beautiful woman and by her not knowing it, only made her that much more alluring.

Tonight, she had curled the ends of her long hair. Her thick tresses fell easily around her shoulders, giving her face that softness and an innocence that had first attracted Jerry to her. She was one of those women who didn't really need makeup, but she had done something with her eye shadow, creating a smokey-eyed look that only added to her attractiveness.

"Why are you looking at me like that?" She set her fork down and wiped her mouth.

"Just admiring your beauty."

She laughed, and a blush bloomed over her cheeks. "Forever the sweet talker."

"What can I say?" He shrugged. "I only speak the truth. Would you like to dance?"

She glanced around the room. "Here?"

"Yeah. Come on." He helped her up, then moved a table that was in front of the sofa. "Right here is good."

Jerry pulled her against his body, one of his hands at the small of her back, and the other holding her hand close to his chest. She draped her free arm around his shoulder as their bodies swayed to the smooth jazz pouring through the Bluetooth speaker.

"Dinner was absolutely delicious. Not as good as the pork tenderloin you made a couple of months ago, but pretty close."

"That's good to hear."

All of the Jenkins men were taught how to cook at a young age, and Jerry was no exception. He never cooked for other women but found pleasure in preparing a meal for Rayne and Stormy. It was just another way for him to take care of his girls, something he loved doing.

"You're full of surprises. Thank you for doing all of this. It means more to me than you know." Since they started dating, Jerry took every opportunity to surprise her and his ladybug. Whether it was a night at the movies, or giving them small gifts, he liked bringing smiles to their faces.

"I'm glad you're enjoying the evening, and just think, the night is still young." He wiggled his eyebrows and she giggled, giving him the response he was after. Finally, she was starting to relax.

He kissed the side of her head, loving how perfectly she fit against him. This was what he'd been missing from his life. Someone to hold. Someone to love. Someone to call his own.

He lowered his mouth to hers as they continued swaying to the beat of the music. He gently coaxed Rayne's lips apart, and his tongue explored the inner recess of her mouth. For the next few minutes, they got lost in each other as he smothered her lips, his need for her growing with each lap of their tongues.

God, this woman. This sweet, desirable woman had him so turned on that he wanted to take her right then and there. But Jerry kept reminding himself. He planned to let her set the pace as far as when they'd take their relationship to the next level. He was ready for what came next, and he had a feeling, she was too.

When the song ended, and another one started, Rayne slowed and started pulling away. Jerry reluctantly released her.

"I'm ready for dessert, now," she said.

"Okay. Let me get the strawberries out of the refrigerator. I'll meet you back at the table."

"Actually, I was thinking about a different type of dessert." Rayne turned her back to him, and lifted her long hair, pulling it over to one shoulder. "Can you unzip me?"

Momentarily surprised, Jerry just stood there until a slow smile spread across his mouth. He chuckled and stepped forward, pleased by her assertiveness.

"It would be my pleasure."

Instead of going right for the zipper, he pulled her back against him and ground against her ass, letting her feel the effect she was already having on him.

Rayne moaned as he littered kisses along the column of her scented neck.

"God, you feel good," he said, still grinding against her as he palmed her ample breasts. She was more than a handful, and Jerry already knew that he was going to have fun exploring her lush body. "Let me get you out of this dress."

When he finally started unzipping her, his breath hitched when he reached the top of her butt and saw the lace strap of the thong.

Unable to resist, he traced a finger down the thin strap, giving it a little tug before allowing it to snap back into place.

"Damn, baby. I wanted to take my time with you tonight, but if the rest of you looks as sexy as this view, I can't make any promises." Each time he looked at her, touched her, rubbed his body against her, he wanted to be buried deep inside of her heat.

"We've waited long enough. I don't want you to go slow tonight," Rayne purred over her shoulder, her gaze meeting his.

"Whatever you want. I'm at your service, but I have to say, the thong kind of caught me off guard."

"I guess you're not the only one with surprises," she cracked, smiling sweetly.

Jerry grinned. "I can see that. And I like what I see."

He zipped the dress the rest of the way down, and Rayne shimmied out of the garment, letting it puddle around her ankles. Jerry held her hand as she stepped out of it.

"Wow," was all he could say as he maintained the hold on her hand. She stood before him in a black, lacy bra and panty set, along with high-heeled sandals looking like every man's fantasy. "You are one sexy ass woman, and I am so glad you're mine."

A shy smile fluttered around her lips, and she lowered her gaze. There was no way in hell he was going to let her shy away from him. She was an erotically attractive woman, and Jerry had every intention of making her feel that way.

"Thank you for the roses and the rose petals," she said when Jerry led her to the bedroom.

While she brushed a few off of the pillows and then sat on the edge of the bed, he started stripping down. He tossed his suit jacket to a nearby chair, and within seconds he was out of the rest of his clothes and left in nothing but his boxer briefs.

Rayne's gaze traveled slowly down his body from the top of his head and didn't stop until she got to his bare feet. She repeated the gesture in reverse, but this time her gaze lingered on his package. And just like that, his dick begged to be free.

"If you keep looking at me like that, this is going to be over way before we get started good." Jerry moved closer. He had waited a long time to have her like this, and her full breasts, toned thighs, and shapely legs taunted him.

He reached behind her back and with a flick of his wrist her bra was unfastened. He dropped it to the floor, and his eyes devoured her gorgeous breasts. Her nipples hardened right before his eyes, and his shaft throbbed at the sight of her.

"Babe." The one word dripped from his tongue moments before Jerry laid her back on the bed. He buried his face between her breasts and squeezed them. Smothered in her softness, her fresh scent engulfed him. "You smell so frickin' good."

Oh, yes. This was what Jerry had been waiting for, what he'd been craving for months.

He lifted his head slightly and his mouth covered one of her nipples. With every swipe and swirl of his tongue over her perky pebbles, her body wiggled beneath him. He couldn't get enough of her breasts.

"Jerry," she moaned, her hand on the back of his head as she continued moving, her lower body bumping against his. As he roused her passion, his grew, and he moved up her body and captured her mouth with his.

She was right. They weren't going to be able to take this first time slow. Not with the erotic sounds she was making and the way she was grinding against him.

His hand slid down the side of her body, over the curve of her hip and to her thigh. Everywhere he touched, he became more engrossed in the softness of her magnificent body.

When Jerry finally pulled his mouth from hers, he gazed into her lust-filled eyes then looked down.

"I love these," he fingered the little strip of lace panties, "but I want you out of them."

Rayne lifted up on her elbows, her chest still heaving. "And though I love how good you look in those," she pointed to his boxer briefs, "I want to see all of you."

The left corner of Jerry's mouth lifted into a half smile. "Your wish is my command."

He climbed off the bed and slid his underwear down his legs while she mirrored his actions by removing her panties and tossing them to the floor. Before returning to the bed, Jerry grabbed a condom from the top drawer of the nightstand where he had stashed them earlier.

He laid next to Rayne, propped up on his elbow, and just the sight of her naked body stretched out on the bed had him about ready to burst. He wanted so bad to take his time and worship every inch of her body, but a surge of excitement pulsed through his veins.

"You are absolutely breathtaking." Jerry hovered above her before lowering his head and capturing her mouth again. He slid his hand between her thighs and ran the pad of his thumb over her slit and Rayne arched against him.

He slid a finger inside of her moist heat, and then added another. "Oh, yeah. You are definitely ready for me."

Rayne whimpered, her thoughts jumbling together.

"Jerry," she gasped, rocking against his hand as his lips moved down the column of her neck while his skilled fingers moved in and out of her. A spark ignited, pushing Rayne close to her release way before she wanted to lose control. But the sweet torture was too much. One powerful thrust later sent her reeling and exploding around his fingers.

Bone weary, Rayne went limp as her chest heaved. She hadn't been with a man in so long but hadn't expected to come that fast. Now, she wanted Jerry inside of her.

With her eyes barely opened, she watched him quickly sheathed himself. He positioned himself between her thighs, nudging them wider with his legs. As he hovered above her, there was a moment when they stared into each other's eyes and something so powerful that Rayne couldn't identify passed between them.

177

"You're mine," Jerry said with raw conviction. "You're all mine."

He eased inside of her and Rayne sucked in a breath and gripped his arms, her nails digging into his skin as her body slowly adjusted to his size.

"Damn…you feel so good." He captured her mouth with his again and started moving slowly, gradually picking up speed.

This was what Rayne wanted. What she needed. His mouth devouring hers. Their tongues tangling. Their bodies moving as one in perfect sync. Yes. This was what her body craved. They'd gone from zero to sixty in a heartbeat, and it had been so long since Rayne had experienced such unrestrained passion.

"Ah, babe," Jerry murmured huskily against her lips.

Heat and raw power radiated off him as he drove in and out of her like an out of controlled eighteen-wheeler flying down a steep hill. Her hands firmly gripped his arms, and she barely hung on as his muscles contracted beneath her touch.

Teetering on the edge of her release, Rayne tried maintaining some control, wanting this to last longer, but she couldn't. The pressure building inside of her was too intense, too strong. After another powerful thrust, she gave herself to him completely. Rayne's release crashed through her body. She bucked uncontrollably against him as wave after wave of pleasure pulsed through her veins.

"Ah, shit, Rayne," Jerry groaned as he pounded in and out of her, going faster and harder before stiffening, then he growled his release. He cursed again, exhaustion on his face as he collapsed on top of her.

Rayne wrapped her arms around his neck and kissed the side of his head, their ragged breathing mingling with the jazz that filtered into the room.

"I'm too heavy," he mumbled before rolling onto his back and pulling her to his side.

Rayne lay there. Her pulse galloped as she stared at the ceiling, feeling as if she had just been transported on a fluffy cloud. "Wow," was all she could manage.

"Wow, indeed."

After a few minutes, once their breathing was somewhat under control, they turned and faced each other.

Jerry pushed a few strands of hair out of her face. "This next time…we take it slow."

Rayne cupped his cheek and smiled. "Well…okay, if you insist."

Chapter Twenty-Three

While on the River Walk boat tour, Rayne reflected on the past week. This was their last day in San Antonio. Everything about the trip had been perfect from the hotel accommodations to her alone time with Jerry. She couldn't have asked for a better trip, a time to get away from her day-to-day life and see San Antonio in a different light.

When Rayne moved away from the city, she had vowed to never look back. She had vowed never to return to the place that had caused her so much pain. She had also vowed that she would never get involved with another man.

Never say never.

Hooking up with Jerry had changed every aspect of her life, and Rayne was glad she had taken a chance on him. She was also glad that they made the trip. Traveling the streets of San Antonio as a tourist, presented her with an opportunity to see the city much differently than she had when living there. They had dined at nice restaurants, visited some of the touristy sights, and she and Jerry had even taken a romantic carriage ride through downtown. A first for Rayne, and she added that experience to the other firsts that she'd had with him.

"And to your left we have the Arneson River Theater," the River Walk cruise tour guide said, explaining how the theater was constructed in 1940, and named after the architect.

It was such a beautiful day, that Rayne could barely concentrate. The calmness of the water during their ride, lulled her into a peaceful state. She closed her eyes and inhaled deeply, taking a few minutes to soak up the sun's rays, loving the feel of the warmth on her skin. The light breeze added to the moment and Rayne realized, she was happier than she'd ever been in her life.

Jerry squeezed her hand which was resting on his thigh, and her eyes flew open. They were packed onto the river boat, shoulder to shoulder with at least fifty other people.

"Did you say something?" she asked.

"No, but you looked as if you had zoned out," he said close to her ear, massaging her neck. Since consummating their relationship, they couldn't keep their hands off of each other.

"Just enjoying the moment." She glanced at Stormy, who was sitting on the other side of Jerry. Her daughter was turning her head back and forth, looking and listening to everything the tour guide said. Like Rayne, no doubt Stormy would be talking about the trip for weeks to come.

Thirty minutes later, when the tour was over, she and Jerry strolled down the street hand-in-hand while Stormy sat on top of his shoulders.

Rayne had mixed emotions about going back home, going back to her reality. For the past week, she had been able to forget about her troubles and just relax. But she couldn't help but wonder what the future held. Yet, she was hopeful that her life was truly turning around for the better.

"Are you guys hungry?" Jerry asked.

"I am. I think I'm hungry for ice cream," Stormy said.

Jerry and Rayne shared a look, smiling at her daughter's constant effort to make ice cream a part of her daily meals.

Still smiling, Rayne returned her attention to the sidewalk in front of them, but slowed when she spotted a familiar face.

She hadn't realized that she had completely stopped in the middle of the sidewalk until Jerry squeezed her hand.

"What's wrong?"

Rayne struggled to get breath into her longs. The person she hadn't seen in years stopped a few feet away.

"Rayne?" Jerry said, concern in his voice as he moved to stand in front of her. "What is it?"

"My sister. I see my sister," she said, hearing the surprise in her own voice.

"Hello, Rayne. It's been a long time." Her sister stood a couple of feet away as if unsure whether to come closer.

Rayne closed the distance between them. "Hi, Liz. It's good seeing you again." And she meant it. The last time they ran into each other, it had been awkward for both of them. "Jerry, this is my sister Elizabeth. Liz, this is my boyfriend, Jerry and my daughter, Stormy."

"Nice to meet you," she said to Jerry. "Stormy...she's gotten so big. She was a baby the last time I saw her."

"You're my mommy's sister?" Stormy said in awe as Jerry lowered her from his shoulders, setting her on her feet. "How old are you?"

"Stormy," Rayne said quickly to ward off another inappropriate question.

"It's okay." Liz laughed, and for the first time that Rayne could remember, she saw some of her facial features in her sister. "I'm thirty-five. How old are you?"

"I'm five, and I'm going to kindergarten pretty soon," Stormy offered. "Do you have any kids?"

"No. Unfortunately, I don't have any children," Liz answered, smiling when she turned to Rayne. "What have you been up to?

"Why don't we step off to the side and get out of traffic," Jerry suggested, holding one of Stormy's hands and his other at the small of Rayne's back.

"Actually, I have a few minutes before I need to be at work, and was heading across the street to the mall. Do you guys have a few minutes." Liz looked at all of them. "For Rayne and me to catch up?"

Rayne glanced at Jerry, who gave a slight nod, but she also saw something else in his gaze. Concern. He probably wondered if Liz was friend or foe, especially since Rayne hadn't told him much about her. She couldn't. She didn't know much about her sister. The foster care system had definitely failed them when they separated them at such a young age. But maybe she could change that.

Rayne gave Jerry a reassuring smile and said to Liz, "We have a little time. Lead the way."

A few minutes later, they were inside the mall. Rayne and Liz sat at a small table in a quiet area, but close enough for her to see Jerry and Stormy. They were at a nearby ice cream parlor.

"It really is good seeing you again, Rayne."

"Same here. I've been thinking about you lately. What have you been up to?"

"Well, I recently finished culinary school, and I'm a sous chef at a restaurant up the street."

Rayne listened as her sister talked about her schooling and long work hours. Unlike the last time they'd run into each other, the conversation didn't feel awkward or forced. They had even exchanged contact information right away, promising to keep in touch with each other.

"Are you still married?" Rayne asked.

"No. I tried marriage twice and each time it ended badly, thanks to me. I pushed them both away with my insecurities. It wasn't until my second husband told me that he couldn't be with someone who couldn't trust him, did I realize I had a problem. He hadn't done anything to make me suspicious of him. Yet, I constantly questioned his whereabouts, who he was with, what he was doing, and the list goes on and on, until he said he had enough."

She gave a slight shrug. "But enough about me. What about you? You said Jerry is your boyfriend. I take it your marriage didn't work out either."

"My husband died a few years ago."

"Oh, I'm sorry to hear that. Is that why you moved to Cincinnati?"

"Yes. I needed a new start," Rayne said without giving any details. If they kept in touch this time, maybe one day she'd share her story.

"Well, Jerry seems nice, and your daughter looks quite taken with him."

"Yeah, he's amazing, and the two of them are almost inseparable."

"Do you think you'll get married again?"

Rayne laughed, her gaze dropping to the handle of her purse that she was playing with. "Had you asked me a year ago, my answer would've been a definite *no*. But now…"

She glanced at Jerry who was sitting at a table with Stormy where they were both eating an ice cream cone. Each time she looked at him, her heart did a little jig inside her chest. Outside of her love for Stormy, she never knew she could love another human being so completely as she did Jerry.

"But now," she returned her attention to Liz, "I would love to get married again."

Chapter Twenty-Four

After dinner, Rayne sat at the kitchen table at the Jenkins' estate, sipping a glass of wine. Sunday brunch was winding down, but the loud talking, arguments, and ribbing was in full effect as people strolled in and out of the kitchen.

Rayne didn't think she would ever get use to the huge, boisterous group, and at times, she was still a little intimidated around them. Having so many people in one place, no matter how big the home, was overwhelming at times. But watching this family was free entertainment at its best.

"I wish I could tell you that they're not always like this, Rayne, but I can't," Katherine Jenkins, the matriarch of the family said, humor dripping from her words. She set her bowl of peach cobbler on the table before sitting next to Violet who was across from Rayne.

The long table sat eight and most of the chairs were filled. Martina, Nick's wife—Sumeera, and a few others sat at the far end in a heated conversation.

"She's right. Sometimes the arguments, or as Martina calls them, *passionate discussions*, get so unruly, they make you want to run out of here," Violet added.

"It's been me and Stormy for so long, it's kind of refreshing to experience the life of a large family."

Katherine laughed. "I'll give you a few more weeks, and then you'll be walking around with ear plugs and trying to find a quiet spot in the house to eat."

Rayne smiled at the older woman. The matriarch was in her eighties and was a prime example of the phrase, *black don't crack*. She had a few laugh lines around her eyes, but other than that, her smooth, dark skin looked healthy and practically glowed. The long, salt and pepper ponytail at the back of her head with tendrils framing her face, created the illusion of a youthful woman.

Despite her age, Katherine moved around her house like someone who was thirty years younger, and still oversaw food preparation for the weekly brunches. This was the third Sunday brunch that Rayne had attended since returning from San Antonio, and she still couldn't get over that they got together weekly.

"Did you get enough to eat?" Violet asked.

"Yes, more than enough. As usual, everything was delicious." Rayne had planned to taste a little bit of everything, but there had been so much to choose from. She ended up settling on shrimp and grits, collard greens, buttermilk hush puppies, and had also tasted some of the brisket which melted in her mouth.

"You must be getting more comfortable around us since Jerry isn't up here hovering over you," Katherine said.

"Yes. I'm getting a little more comfortable," Rayne responded.

Just the mention of Jerry sent butterflies fluttering inside of Rayne's stomach. It was a feeling that she never wanted to lose. Every day with him brought more joy to her life than she ever could have imagine.

She loved being anywhere he was, but tried to give him space around his family. Normally, when attending the brunch, the three of them ate together. This Sunday was different. Jerry had decided to eat with the guys on the lower level in the theater room. The Cincinnati Bengals were playing the Pittsburgh Steelers and supposedly it was a game none of them could miss.

Stormy also had her own plans. Rayne might still be getting used to the group, but her daughter was in her element around people. Since some of Jerry's cousins had children her age, she spent most of her visit eating and playing with them.

"Rayne, how's the new job?" Sumeera asked, slowly moving to the seat next to Rayne. She shifted in the chair, probably trying to get comfortable, and rubbed her protruding belly. She was seven months pregnant but looked as if she would give birth any day now. "I figured I'd ask, because the twin has been going on and on about how amazing you are."

The *twin* was Nate, Nick's twin brother. He was the one who had recently gotten married. Though Rayne knew the moment she saw them together that they were brothers, she hadn't realized right away that they were twins. They weren't identical, but definitely looked alike.

"The job is great. I absolutely love the work, and I couldn't ask for better bosses."

She reported to Nate mostly, but he owned the property development company with his Uncle Ben. Rayne had been hired as their administrative assistant, shortly after returning from San Antonio. She enjoyed that type of work so much that she was switching her major from psychology to business management.

In addition to the new job, Rayne had found an accelerated college degree program that would accept the credits she already had. It turned out that she had more credits than she originally thought and should finish the program in less than a year.

Moments later, Nate strolled into the kitchen carrying dirty dishes, and Nick was right behind him.

"Oh good. I'm glad you two are going to get started with clean up," Katherine said. She had a large clean-up schedule hanging on the wall in the over-sized pantry. It had each

Sunday of the month listed, along with who was responsible for cleaning the kitchen after brunch.

Rayne stood, and gathered some of the dirty dishes that were on the table. Jerry was also on the clean-up schedule. Maybe if she helped, they could head home a little earlier than usual.

"I take it the game is over?" she asked, setting the dishes on the counter next to the sink where Nate was standing.

"Yeah, and Jerry should be up soon. I thought he was right behind me."

"Hey, Nate. I was just about to head downstairs to see you," Martina said, adding to the pile of dishes near the sink. "I heard that Liberty is having morning sickness. So what, you marry her one day and then impregnate her the next? What's up with that? And why y'all tryin' to keep it a secret?"

The murderous look Nate gave his cousin could've cut through stone, but who could blame him? Rayne would be pissed too if someone blurted out something about her that she wasn't ready to share.

"I think we need a new rule for Sunday brunch," Nate said to no one in particular, but loud enough for everyone to hear. "Martina Jenkins-Kendricks, shouldn't be allowed on the premises without Paul. If he's out of town, she should either go with him or stay home. Now, can I get someone to second that motion?"

"Whatever, just answer the questions and keep my man out of this," she snapped.

Rayne had only met the former U.S. senator twice, but did notice a difference in Martina whenever Paul was around. She was gentler and usually hung out wherever he was in the house. Anyone who saw them together would know immediately how much they loved each other.

"Rayne, you'll soon learn that secrets aren't safe around our resident troublemaker," Nate said. "And to answer your question, MJ, yes. She's eight weeks pregnant."

"Who's pregnant?" Christina asked, as she and Nick strolled into the kitchen, their hands filled with serving dishes. "I only caught the tail end of the conversation."

"Nate was just confirming that Liberty is pregnant." Martina organized the leftover food and grabbed Styrofoam carryout containers from the pantry. Their grandmother insisted that everyone take some of the leftovers home with them.

"I thought you guys weren't telling anyone until after the first trimester," Nick rolled up his sleeves as he approached the sink.

"That was the plan," Nate murmured then turned his back to the group and started loading one of the two dishwashers.

Martina put her hands on her hips. "So that makes three who will be having babies in the next seven or eight months."

"Three?" Sumeera asked. "Me, Liberty and who else?"

Everyone looked around and their eyes landed on Rayne.

She stepped back with her hands up. "Uh, don't look at me."

Toni-Jenkins Logan ambled into the kitchen wearing a *This Girl is the World's Greatest Plumber* T-shirt and headed to the kitchen table. "Gram, do you still have some of that ginger tea?"

"Wait! Oh my God! You're the one who's pregnant?" Christina shrieked and hurried over to a stunned Toni and hugged her.

Katherine and Violet shook their heads smiling. It was safe to say they already knew.

"Dang, MJ. Yo butt can't keep nothin'!" Toni snapped, but accepted the hugs and well wishes from her family.

After hugging Toni, Rayne left to go in search of Jerry. The noise level in the kitchen had reached new heights.

This was her new life...and she loved her adopted family, drama and all. Funny what a difference a few months could make. The carjacking, injuries and even the layoff from the factory seemed like a lifetime ago, though it was only a couple of months. Those memories didn't overshadow the joy radiating inside of her.

Never in a million years would Rayne have guessed that moving to Cincinnati would end up being the best decision she ever made. Each day, her future looked brighter and brighter.

Chapter Twenty-Five

Moments ago, there had been at least twenty guys watching the game. Now Jerry and Luke were the last two in the theater room. Most had gone to the large game room that was just outside the door, while some of the others had headed up stairs.

"Luke, I need a favor," Jerry said to his brother-in-law.

"And what's that?" he asked, sitting back in one of the leather chairs watching another football game, looking as if he didn't have a care in the world.

"I need you to switch clean up days with me."

Luke started shaking his head before any words came out of his mouth. "Nope, because the moment I need to switch, your ass probably won't be here."

"You act as if I ask you to switch all the time. This is a first, and I promise I won't ask again."

Jerry stood and pulled his ringing phone out of his pocket. When he saw that it was Pilar, one of their customers calling, he silenced the phone. He rarely talked to any of their customers if he was off duty. In the voice message she left the other day, she had asked that he give her a call back regarding one of the jobs they were doing for her. When he called, he got her voice message and they'd been playing phone tag ever since.

"Come on, Luke. Help me out here. I need to go and take care of something."

Jerry wasn't sure what Luke heard in his voice, but he turned to look at him.

"Why? What are you up to? And who the hell keeps blowing up your phone?"

"Nobody. Just a customer who I've been playing phone tag with."

Luke sat forward and narrowed his eyes at Jerry. "If your ass is screwing around on Rayne, I'm going to kick your motherfu—"

"Whoa! What the hell, man? How we go from me asking you to fill in for me upstairs, to you thinking I'm stepping out on my woman?"

Now Luke was standing, his arms folded across his chest. They were close in height and build, but Jerry was pretty sure his brother-in-law could probably kick his ass. There was a reason Martina referred to the guy as the *thug lawyer*. Luke had more swagger and brains than anyone Jerry knew, but there was an underlying edginess about him that would make even a badass tread lightly.

"So, the phone calls are not some type of hook up with another woman?"

"No. Definitely not! I love Rayne more than life. There's no way in hell I'm going to mess up what we have for some tail. You can believe that!"

"Then why do you need me to fill in for you?"

"Because I need to talk to Rayne and it might take a little while."

Seconds ticked by while Luke studied him as if trying to determine if he was telling the truth.

"All right, but you have to fill in for me twice," he said.

"Deal."

They both headed for the door but pulled up short when they saw Rayne in the doorway.

How much had she heard? Jerry did a mental rewind of the conversation he and Luke just had and decided that they hadn't said anything out of line. If Rayne was still standing there, she had heard him profess his love for her.

"I'm gonna head up," Luke said to Jerry, then greeted Rayne before clearing out.

She acknowledged Luke, but her gaze was on Jerry. "Hey," she said. "I was just wondering where you were."

"I was actually on my way upstairs to get you." He brushed a quick kiss across her lips. "Come with me." He reached for her hand and gently pulled her along with him up the stairs.

"Where are we going?" she asked as they passed the family room, dining room, and headed toward the front of the house.

"You'll see."

His grandparents' estate was one of his favorite places in the world. Seeing all of the family photos lining the walls of the hallway, brought back fond memories of him and his cousins playing hide-go-seek. The house had hosted more parties and celebrations than some hotel ballrooms, but they didn't always have all of this.

Recently, Jerry's mother had told Rayne about his grandparents humbled beginnings. She shared one story after another, some that he hadn't even heard before. It reminded him how hard his grandparents had worked and sacrificed to create a legacy for their family.

"In here," Jerry said when they arrived at his grandfather's study. He glanced in and made sure no one was in there before he ushered Rayne in. His grandfather and some of Jerry's uncles were hanging out in the carriage house near the pool, probably smoking cigars. Something his grandmother didn't approve of.

Jerry released Rayne's hand as he closed and locked the door, but when he turned, she had taken a few steps back, uncertainty in her eyes.

His heart plummeted to his stomach as that uncertainty he had just seen in her eyes turned to defiance.

Okay, maybe I need to rethink this idea.

Rayne folded her arms across her chest, bringing attention to her enticing breasts. The low-cut blouse she had on revealed just enough cleavage to make him want to take her on top of his grandfather's desk.

"Jerry, I am not having sex with you in here!" she hissed as if reading his mind. "Anyone could walk in."

Relief flooded through is body, and he burst out laughing, understanding why she would be concerned. Since leaving San Antonio, he hadn't been able to get enough of her. Every rare moment they had alone, he found places to make love to her. During dinner at his parents' house one night, he had even snuck her into his old bedroom to test out his old bed. And then there was that one Sunday, during one of the brunches, that they stole away into an upstairs bathroom.

That was fun.

But she had the wrong idea.

He approached her and slid his arm around her waist. "Though that idea of making love to you in here appeals to me," he nuzzled her scented neck, loving the way she squirmed against him, "that's not why I brought you in here."

When her shoulders sagged and her defenses went back down, Jerry kissed her cheek and guided her across the room. They went past his grandfather's large desk, and didn't stop until they were in the sitting area. Jerry directed her to the brown, leather sofa.

"Have a seat." Once she was seated, he sat next to her, thinking about all that he wanted to say.

"Jerry, you're scaring me. What is it? Does this have anything to do with the conversation you and Luke were having a little while ago? *Is* there someone else?"

"No. Absolutely not, and just like I told Luke, I'm not risking what you and I have for anyone. Sweetheart, I love *you.* I don't want anyone else, and if it takes the rest of my life to prove that to you, then that's exactly what I intend to do."

Jerry held her left hand between his. "I know we've only been dating a few months," he started, his pulse picking up in speed with each word, "but I knew way before then that I wanted to spend the rest of my life with you."

He released her hand and dug the velvet box from his pocket before getting down on one knee.

"Oh. My. God," she breathed and covered her mouth with her hands.

"You said that you would never get married again, but I'm asking you to please reconsider. I have worked like hell to become the man you deserve, a man who will cherish you for the rest of our lives. I know that you and Ladybug are a package deal, and if you'll have me, I promise to be the best father she could ever want. Rayne, will you marry me?"

She nodded, tears filling her eyes. "Oh, Jerry. I love you, too. And yes, yes I'll marry you!"

Jerry slipped the three-carat, pear shaped diamond ring onto her finger and pulled her into a standing position. Cupping Rayne's face, he kissed her with everything within him, wanting her to feel the love that he felt deep inside.

"Are you're sure about this?" Jerry asked when he lifted his head, wanting to make sure she wasn't feeling pressured to say yes.

"I'm more than sure. I can't wait to marry you."

After another quick kiss, he said, "Come on. Let's go let everybody know the good news."

A few minutes later, they stood just inside the huge family room where much of the family had gathered.

"Stormy," Jerry called out, and her head popped up. She and Janay were playing a board game in front of the television. "Come here, baby. And may I have everyone's attention."

Stormy ran to them, and everyone stopped their conversations.

"Rayne and I have an announcement to make," he said, holding her hand tighter. "We're getting married!"

Instead of the cheers and congratulatory responses he expected, all they got were wide-eyed stares. No one moved.

No one spoke. They just looked at them as if seeing him and Rayne for the first time.

Then everyone started talking at once.

"You owe me twenty dollars," Martina said to Toni.

"I think she's good for him, but I can't believe she said yes," someone else chimed in.

"It's about time that boy settles down," came another response.

"Hey! I'm standing right here!" Jerry shouted good-naturedly, not surprised by the wise cracks.

Stormy looked at him and Rayne, confusion on her sweet face. Jerry watched as that confusion morphed into understanding.

"Mommy, you're getting married?" she asked in a rush, her excitement slowly building.

"Yes, sweetheart. Jerry and I are getting married."

"Yay!" She screeched, bouncing up and down and turning in circles in front of them. "I'm so excited. I'm getting a daddy! I'm getting a daddy! Thank you, mommy!" She slammed into Rayne, and wrapped her arms around her mother's legs. "I'm so happy."

Jerry chuckled, then picked up Stormy.

"My wish came true," she said on a sob, but quickly wiped her eyes and smiled. "I wanted you to be my daddy."

Jerry's heart melted each time he looked into those beautiful eyes that were identical to her mother's. He kissed her cheek. "I am so happy you're going to be my little girl."

"Me too." She hugged him tightly before he put her down.

For a few minutes, they basked in the well wishes and soaked up all of the hugs from his family. His parents were the last ones to approach them.

"I'm proud of you son," Jerry's father said, pulling him into a bear hug. Thomas Jenkins wasn't a big talker, but had always been quick to tell and show his kids how much he loved them.

"Thanks, Dad."

His father hugged Rayne and whispered something to her.

Then Violet wrapped her arms around Jerry and Rayne at the same time. "I'm so happy for you kids, and Rayne, you were already my daughter, but I'm glad you two are making it official."

"Aw, Violet," Rayne cooed, hugging his mother firmly. "You are so special to me. Thank you for everything."

Jerry noticed how choked up Rayne was, and he pulled her to his side while he got everyone's attention again.

"I have one more surprise," he announced.

Rayne's perfectly arched eyebrows lifted in question, but all Jerry did was smile.

"Martina, can you bring in the surprise?"

"Sure." She left the room and a few minutes later, returned with a huge box. She walked slowly across the room and set it on the floor near Stormy.

"What is it?" Stormy asked as she and Janay crowded around it.

"Something for you and Janay to play with," Jerry said and carefully lifted the box to reveal the custom-made doll house.

Gasps went up around the room.

Instead of Stormy's usual exuberant bouncing around, she stood frozen with her mouth hanging open.

"That is absolutely beautiful," Rayne breathed.

It had been hard keeping it a secret from her. Jerry had planned to save the gift for Christmas, but when Martina told him that it was already done, he couldn't wait.

"It's a doll house," Stormy finally said, clearly astonished by the gift. "It looks just like my mommy and daddy's houses."

Now Jerry was the one stunned into silence. His heart was so full. He didn't think he would ever get used to her calling him daddy.

Stormy walked over and hugged him. "Thank you, daddy. I love it, and I love you," she said.

"I love you too," Jerry said around the lump in his throat.

This would definitely go down as one of the best days of his life.

Chapter Twenty-Six

"What's up, Boss Man?" Jerry asked when he ambled into Nick's office and found him sitting at the round, meeting table that was in the corner.

"Not much. Thanks for coming in. Where's Rayne? I thought you guys were stopping here in between looking at houses."

"We are. We told the real estate agent that we would meet her at the next house in a couple of hours." Jerry joined him at the table. "And Rayne's downstairs. MJ is giving her a tour of the carpenter shop, as well as some of the others."

"That's cool. I'm surprised she hadn't been by here before today."

"She has, but I never took the time to give her a tour of the whole building."

Nick nodded. "Oh, I see. Well, what I called you in for is that I wanted to let you know that the foreman's position is yours if you want it."

"Yeah!" Jerry did a Tiger Woods fist pump but tried to maintain some cool by staying in his seat. "Of course, I want the job."

He had interviewed for the position a few weeks ago. They might've been family, but Nick always treated the business like a business. He would never just slide someone into a position. He didn't care who you were. You had to be qualified and be a good fit.

"Your first day as foremen is in two weeks. Ted will train you during the first week. After that you're on your own. But I think it'll be a smooth transition since you know just as much as he does about the trade and the job."

For thirty minutes, they discussed next steps, the position and a few of the jobs coming up. With this promotion and his engagement, Jerry's life plans were lining up perfectly. He couldn't wait to share the news with Rayne.

Nick's intercom buzzed, and he left the table. Pushing the green button on his desk phone, he said, "Yes."

"Hey, Nick. Mrs. Brooks is here."

Nick's brows dipped into a frown. "Does she have an appointment?"

"No, but she says it's important that she meets with you because she doesn't want to hold up the job any longer. She says—"

"Tam, just escort her upstairs. Thanks."

Jerry stood. "I guess that's my cue to make a move."

"Actually, stick around. Mrs. Brooks had questions about a fixture for her home office and some for the bathrooms that we're remodeling. When Ted leaves, this job will fall into your lap if it isn't done by then."

A few minutes later, Mrs. Brooks strolled into the office, but what shocked Jerry was seeing Dana with her. Though Dana had been blowing up his phone shortly after that run-in at her parent's house, he hadn't heard or seen her in the last few months.

Right now, with the way she was dressed and how she carried herself, Dana looked like a multi-millionaire who owned a Fortune 500 company. Instead, she owned a small marketing firm up the street, but that didn't mean she looked any less professional. Her flattering shoulder-length bob bounced with every step she took, and the stylish, gray pants suit molded perfectly over her full-figured body. She was definitely a looker.

"Hello, Mrs. Brooks," Nick said, snagging Jerry's attention.

"Hi, Nick. Thanks for agreeing to see me. I won't take up too much of your time."

Dana smiled at Jerry, but didn't speak right away. Like usual, whenever she saw him, her appreciative gaze slid down his body.

I am definitely going to have to make it clear that I'm not interested or available.

"It's good to see you again, Jerry," Dana purred, her ruby-red lips tilting up into a seductive smile as she laid her hand on his arm.

If it were anyone else, he wouldn't think much of the way she touched his arm or his back whenever she talked to him. But the lust radiating in her eyes, and the vibe he was picking up on, let him know that she didn't care that he was involved with someone. Before, when he told her that he wasn't interested, his feelings for Rayne were somewhat one-sided. Now that they were engaged, he definitely had to make it clear to Dana where they stood.

"You two know each other?" Mrs. Brooks asked, taking the seat that Nick pulled out for her.

"Yes, we're good friends and go way back," Dana said sweetly before Jerry could speak. She said it with just a little too much seduction for his taste.

"Oh, how nice," her mother said. "It's such a small world."

"Yes, it is," Jerry murmured. He glanced at Nick who was looking at him, probably wondering exactly how he knew Dana.

"What can I do for you, Mrs. Brooks?" Nick asked, reclaiming his seat once Dana was seated.

"I know you want your people to finish up the second phase of our renovation, but there are a few changes I wanted to make to the plans first," she said.

For the next thirty minutes, she went back and forth on what type of flooring she wanted for her house. She was also still undecided about fixtures.

"Jerry probably can give you some direction on the light fixtures," Nick said.

"Mrs. Brooks, why don't you show me the bathroom fixture that you and your husband are leaning toward," Jerry said.

"Don't you want to sit down?" Dana asked Jerry and patted the seat next to her.

"No, I'm good. I'm only here for a few more minutes anyway. All right, Mrs. Brooks, show me which fixtures you're thinking of going with before I leave. As Nick said, our guys will be ready to install them this coming week." He leaned over her shoulder and looked at the web page that she pulled up.

"I changed my mind about having the euro design ceiling fan in my home office. I think this chandelier would be fabulous in the space."

"You're right, that chandelier would look nice in your office, but I wouldn't recommend it," Jerry said. "I'm actually surprised it's still on the market. The bulbs it takes are almost impossible to find, and it's also a pain to change those bulbs."

"And what about the one she picked for the bathrooms?" Nick asked.

For the next few minutes, they discussed other options for the home office, as well as the bathroom fixtures. By the time Jerry was done highlighting the pros and cons of a few possibilities, she finally nailed down her choices.

Dana lunged out of her seat and threw her arms around his neck. "Thanks for helping my mother. I'm glad you were here."

Jerry eased out of her hold and put a little distance between them. "I'm glad to be of help. I'll get one of our guys to place the order today, and we should receive them in a couple of days." He glanced at his watch. "Well, it was good seeing you both again, but I need to get going."

Nick gave him a head nod. "Thanks for coming in, man."

"Actually, I need to talk to you about something," Dana said in a rush, gathering her belongings. "Mom, I'll meet you outside."

Once in the hallway, Jerry got in her face. "What the hell was that in there?"

"That was me showing my appreciation, but I'd rather show you in a different way. Your place or mine?"

*

Rayne rode the elevator to the top floor, fascinated by all that she'd seen of Jenkins & Sons. She knew the company was successful, but what she'd seen had exceeded her expectations. To say she was impressed with what the Jenkins family had created would be putting it mildly.

Exiting the elevator, Rayne wandered down the hall. She nodded at two guys who were talking near an office door and then gave a slight wave at a man she had seen earlier in the paint shop. If she remembered correctly, Nick's office was around the corner.

Rayne made the last right turn but stopped a short distance from where she saw Jerry and a woman talking. Part of her considered backing up and giving them some privacy since the woman was probably a client considering how well she was dressed. But there was something about the way she was looking at Jerry, that gave Rayne pause.

"Listen, Dana. I don't know what part of *not interested* you don't understand, but you and me—never gonna happen again."

"I've missed you," she said as if not hearing him. "How about you come by my place tonight. I'll cook dinner, and then you can show me how much you've missed me."

"That's not going to happen," Rayne said before she could stop herself, anger clawing through her veins. Jerry spun around as she walked toward them. "He's not available. Not tonight. Not tomorrow. Not ever."

The words flew from her mouth with a boldness Rayne never knew she had. This wasn't her. She rarely confronted people, but that was before she had a man worth fighting for.

"Excuse me? Who the hell do you think—"

"Whoa. Hold up, Dana." Jerry put his arm around Rayne. "This is my fiancée and I sure as hell ain't gon' let you talk to her any kind of way," he said, an edge in his voice that Rayne hadn't heard before.

"Fiancée?" She looked Rayne up and down and turned up her nose as if smelling something bad. "Honey, clearly you don't know who you're dealing with. He ain't—"

"Actually, I know exactly who I'm dealing with. He's the man I'm going to marry," Rayne told her, then turned her attention to Jerry. "Ready to go?"

"Yeah." He kissed her lips and looked at Dana. "Lose my number."

She made a dismissive sound in the back of her throat. "You'll be back." She stomped past them, and they watched until she was out of sight.

"Jerry, please tell me I'm not going to have to deal with more women like her."

He cupped her face between his hands. "You're *never* going to have to deal with women like her as it relates to me. She's from my past, but it was never anything serious. I hope you know that you have nothing to worry about. I'm all yours."

In her heart, Rayne knew that, but every now and then doubts snuck in and brought up memories of Kirk and his betrayal. She never again wanted to miss signs that her man was cheating.

Jerry lifted her chin, forcing her to meet his eyes. "I'm serious, Rayne. I would never cheat on you," he said as if reading her mind. "We're getting married, and we're going to have an amazing life together. You don't *ever* have to worry about me stepping out on you or letting anyone come between us."

Rayne believed him, and she had no intention of letting anyone come between them either. He was hers, and she was his.

"I love you so much. I can't wait to be your wife."

"And I can't wait to spend the rest of my life with you."

Epilogue

Nine months later…

A smile lifted the corners of Rayne's mouth as she stared out over the backyard. She admired the huge patio, the custom-made swing set, and the start of a vegetable garden that she had always dreamed of having one day.

Had anyone told her a year ago that she would be married and living in her dream home, Rayne would've laughed in their face. She was living proof that anything was possible when you don't give up.

Don't let your circumstances control you.

Almost daily, Violet's words played through Rayne's mind. She didn't know what she would've done without her mother-in-law or the Jenkins clan all those months ago. Jerry and his family had changed her life, supported her in every way and welcomed her and Stormy into their world. Because of their love, Rayne walked in a peace she never knew existed.

I am so blessed.

She turned away from the sliding patio door and went back into the kitchen to finish breakfast. They had moved into the four-bedroom, three-and-a-half-bathroom house two months ago and some days Rayne felt as if she was living someone else's life. The chef's kitchen with its stone-gray cabinets, marble countertops, and top of the line stainless steel appliances, was her favorite room in the house. Her heart sang each time she walked into the space.

Rayne opened the top oven to check on the French toast casserole, deciding to give it a few more minutes before she took it out. Jerry had left early to check on a job and she had promised to have breakfast ready by the time he returned.

Once Rayne finished the bacon, eggs, and removed the casserole from the oven, she heard the overhead garage door go up and the rumble of Jerry's truck.

A few minutes later, the kitchen door that led to the garage opened.

"Psst."

She glanced over her shoulder and frowned. Jerry stood in the doorway, peeking into the kitchen before looking left and right. He wore the same sneaky expression that he had when he came home one day after work and said, *I found your dream home.*

Rayne narrowed her eyes. "What are you up to?"

"Where's Ladybug?"

"She's upstairs playing. Why?"

He strolled into the house, closing the door behind him. "Because I have a surprise for her."

Rayne shook her head. "Jerry, you're going to spoil her if you keep buying her stuff."

"My little girl deserves to be spoiled."

The last surprise had been when he, his father and Liam built the mini playground in the back yard. Rayne couldn't even imagine what else he had up his sleeve. But in all honesty, she couldn't have picked a better father for her daughter or a better husband for herself.

Married six months ago at the Jenkins' family estate, they had only invited the immediate family, wanting to keep the wedding relatively small. They ended up with over seventy guests, but the backyard wedding still felt intimate and had been absolutely gorgeous. It was hands down one of the best days of Rayne's life.

"How are you feeling this morning, Mrs. Jenkins?"

Standing behind Rayne, Jerry wrapped his arms around her waist. As usual, her heart rate galloped whenever he was in her presence, and being in his arms was her favorite place to be.

"I feel pretty good." Rayne laid her head back against his hard chest, savoring their quiet moment.

He placed his large hand on her belly. "How's my boy doing?"

As if knowing his father's voice, the baby moved, and Jerry sucked in a breath. "That will never get old. Just amazing," he said in awe.

She placed her hand on top of his. "Yeah, the miracle of life is pretty remarkable."

Rayne loved that she could share something so special with this wonderful man. In less than four months, they would welcome a new addition to the Jenkins family, and she could hardly wait to meet their baby boy.

Jerry nuzzled her neck, and Rayne shivered. The heady sensation of his skilled lips against her heated skin took her desire for him to new levels. And unless she wanted their breakfast to get cold, she needed to put on the brakes before they got too carried away.

She wiggled against him, a weak attempt at breaking out of his hold, but Jerry held firm.

"Where you tryin' to go?" he said, his voice muffled against the column of her neck.

"I just don't want you to start nothing we can't finish right now."

"Mmm," he moaned, nipping and kissing her neck, ignoring her words. "Have I mentioned how much I love you?"

"Everyday. You show me too. Have I mentioned how much I love you, and how blessed I feel to have you as my husband?"

"Um, yeah. You might've mentioned it a few times."

Rayne turned in his arms and cupped his face before kissing his sexy lips. "Let's talk about this surprise you have for Stormy. Should I be concerned?"

"Nope. You have nothing to worry about."

She leaned back and searched his dark eyes. "Okay, let me rephrase that question. Should I be concerned that you spent too much money?"

"Nope, but do me a favor. Call her down here, and you guys meet me in the family room."

"Can whatever this is wait? Breakfast is going to get cold."

"It won't take long. Come on, just get her into the family room." He kissed Rayne again before releasing her, then headed to the garage while she went to the stairs.

"Stormy, your dad is here," Rayne called out.

Little feet pounded overhead. "Hey, Daddy! You're back." Stormy hurried down the stairs. "Are we still going to the... Where is he?" she asked, running into the kitchen and then looking out back.

"He said for us to meet him in the family room."

Stormy ran ahead of her and hopped onto the leather sofa sectional. "Did he buy me something?" she asked, jumping up and down on the furniture.

"I don't know, but sit down before you fall."

"Ladybug, close your eyes," Jerry said from somewhere nearby, but he stayed out of sight.

"Okay." Stormy squealed as if he had already given her the surprise. Rayne smiled, not wanting to admit that she was a little curious and excited, too.

Jerry walked in, and Rayne's mouth dropped open. "Jerry," she said, the warning in her tone made it clear that she wasn't happy about his surprise, but all he did was grin.

"Can I open my eyes now?" Stormy asked, her voice an octave higher than moments ago.

"Yeah, baby. Open your eyes."

Stormy screamed and leaped off the sofa. "You got me a puppy! I can't believe it. You got me a puppy. I'm so excited!" She hopped up and down. "Thank you, Daddy!"

"You're welcome."

"Can I hold him? What's his name?" Questions flew from her mouth as Jerry got down on the floor with the shy, tiny Labrador retriever.

Rayne walked across the room. She wanted to be pissed that he hadn't discussed this with her, but her daughter's excitement wiped out any misgivings about them getting a puppy.

Stormy struggled to pick up the beautiful animal.

"Here let me help you. *She's* a little shy." Jerry scooped up the puppy and set her in Stormy's arms. "She's still a baby, Ladybug. We're going to have to teach her right from wrong, make sure she doesn't put the wrong things in her mouth, clean up after her, and most importantly, we have to love on her, okay?"

Stormy bobbed her head up and down, gently hugging the puppy. "I love her so much. What's her name?"

Jerry knelt on the floor, staying close to her and the puppy. "What would you like to name her?"

"Umm...I'm going to call her Sunshine. Hi, Sunshine," she cooed.

Rayne smiled at how affectionate Stormy was being and the name choice. Considering her child's sunny disposition, she's the one who should've been named Sunshine.

"Why don't we put Sunshine down so she can start getting used to her new home.

Stormy followed the puppy around the room as Rayne and Jerry looked on.

"Shouldn't we have discussed this little surprise?" Rayne asked him, unable to stop herself from petting the gorgeous puppy.

"Probably, but I couldn't resist. Look at her."

"Yeah, she is cute."

"I just thought of something," Jerry said, holding Rayne's hand and guiding her to the sofa. "Now I live with a Rayne, Stormy, and a Sunshine. I wonder what's next, Windy?"

Rayne laughed and elbowed him in the side. "I see you have jokes."

He grinned and put his arms around her shoulders, pulling her close. "Our family is growing," he said quietly as they watched Stormy play with the puppy.

"Yeah, it is." She draped her arms across his midsection and laid her head on his shoulder. "Thank you for giving me a family."

Jerry placed a lingering kiss on her forehead. "And thank you for taking a chance on me."

Rayne looked up at him. "That was the best decision I ever made. I love you so much."

He lowered his head, and his mouth stopped inches from hers. "And I love you more, Mrs. Jenkins."

*

If you enjoyed this book by Sharon C. Cooper,
consider leaving a review on any online book site, review site or social media outlet.

Join Sharon's Mailing List

To get sneak peeks of upcoming stories and to hear about giveaways that Sharon is sponsoring, visit www.sharoncooper.net to join her mailing list.

About the Author

Award-winning and bestselling author, Sharon C. Cooper, is a romance-a-holic - loving anything that involves romance with a happily-ever-after, whether in books, movies, or real life. Sharon writes contemporary romance, as well as romantic suspense and enjoys rainy days, carpet picnics, and peanut butter and jelly sandwiches. She's been nominated for numerous awards and is the recipient of an Emma Award for Romantic Suspense of the Year 2015 (Truth or Consequences), Emma Award - Interracial Romance of the Year 2015 (All You'll Ever Need), and BRAB (book club) Award -Breakout Author of the Year 2014. When Sharon is not writing or working, she's hanging out with her amazing husband, doing volunteer work or reading a good book (a romance of course). To read more about Sharon and her novels, visit www.sharoncooper.net

Connect with Sharon Online:
Website: http://sharoncooper.net
Facebook:
http://www.facebook.com/AuthorSharonCCooper21?ref=hl
Twitter: https://twitter.com/#!/Sharon_Cooper1
Subscribe to her blog: http://sharonccooper.wordpress.com/
Goodreads:
http://www.goodreads.com/author/show/5823574.Sharon_
C_Cooper
Pinterest: https://www.pinterest.com/sharonccooper/

Other Titles

Atlanta's Finest Series

Vindicated (book 1)

Indebted (book 2)

Accused (book 3)

Jenkins & Sons Construction Series (Contemporary Romance)

Love Under Contract

Proposal for Love

A Lesson on Love

Unplanned Love – *Coming Soon*

Jenkins Family Series (Contemporary Romance)

Best Woman for the Job (Short Story Prequel)

Still the Best Woman for the Job (book 1)

All You'll Ever Need (book 2)

Tempting the Artist (book 3)

Negotiating for Love (book 4)

Seducing the Boss Lady (book 5)

Love at Last (Holiday Novella)

When Love Calls (Novella)

Reunited Series (Romantic Suspense)

Blue Roses (book 1)

Secret Rendezvous (Prequel to Rendezvous with Danger)

Rendezvous with Danger (book 2)

Truth or Consequences (book 3)

Operation Midnight (book 4)

Stand Alones

Something New ("Edgy" Sweet Romance)

Legal Seduction (Harlequin Kimani – Contemporary Romance)

Sin City Temptation (Harlequin Kimani – Contemporary Romance)

A Dose of Passion (Harlequin Kimani – Contemporary Romance)

Model Attraction (Harlequin Kimani – Contemporary Romance)

A Passionate Kiss (Bennett Triplets Series)

www.ingramcontent.com/pod-product-compliance
Lightning Source LLC
Chambersburg PA
CBHW032000240626
47153CB00003B/1049